DR. SAKETHA Q. ADAMS

On the Bathroom Floor

First edition

ISBN (paperback): 979-8-9999165-0-1
ISBN (hardcover): 979-8-9999165-1-8

This book was professionally typeset on Reedsy.
Find out more at reedsy.com

Contents

Foreword

From the outside looking in, she was the epitome of success. Intelligent, articulate, driven – a woman who seemed to effortlessly navigate the complexities of life with grace and poise. Society had painted a picture of a woman firmly in control, a leader, someone who had it all figured out.

But beneath the polished veneer, in the quiet solitude of a tiled floor, lay a different truth. The bathroom floor became her sanctuary, a cold, hard space where the carefully constructed walls of her composure could finally crumble. It was there, amidst the silent sobs and whispered prayers, that a profound realization dawned. She was not alone.

Looking beyond her own pain, she saw them – reflections of herself in countless other intelligent, accomplished women. Women who, by society's standards, also had it all. Yet, they too found themselves on that same unforgiving surface, victims of heartbreak, betrayal, and the crushing weight of relationships gone wrong.

What she witnessed was a poignant and often unspoken reality: the silent sacrifice of self that many intelligent women make in the name of love. The subtle, and sometimes not-so-subtle, act of "dummying down" their brilliance, their strength, their very essence, to soothe the fragile egos of their spouses or significant others. A heartbreaking dance of diminishing oneself to empower another.

This book is not just the author's story; it is the story of so many. It peels back the layers of societal expectation and reveals the raw vulnerability that lies beneath even the most accomplished exteriors. It is a journey through the darkness of heartbreak, a testament to the power of female solidarity, and a beacon of hope for those who have found themselves seeking solace on that cold, hard floor.

Prepare to be moved, to recognize yourself or someone you know within these pages, and to ultimately discover the strength that lies in embracing our true selves, even when the world expects us to be someone else. This is a story that needed to be told, and it is told with unflinching honesty and a profound understanding of the complexities of the human heart.

Preface

For years, I believed that success was a mask you had to wear.

I built a life and a career that, by every outward measure, looked perfect. I was the capable, confident, and meticulously organized professional—the woman who always had it all together. This mask, I believed, was not optional; it was the essential armor required to climb higher and stay on top. But behind the scenes, away from the accolades and the admiration, I was quietly falling apart.

My own breakdown wasn't the most profound realization; it was the chilling discovery that I was not alone. Everywhere I looked, I saw women just like me—brilliant, accomplished, and confident on the outside—battling their own internal crises, all in silent isolation. We were a hidden sisterhood of women collapsing behind closed doors, convinced our struggles were ours to bear alone.

I was inspired to write "On the Bathroom Floor" because I lived it. I understand the intense pressure to maintain an image of perfection, and I know the exhaustion that comes with the performance. This book is my attempt to pull back the curtain on that secret world. I wrote it to start a vital conversation and to shatter the dangerous myth that vulnerability is a sign of weakness.

My journey isn't just about the collapse; it's about the breakthrough that followed. It is about reframing that solitary moment on the bathroom floor not as a sign of failure, but as a sacred opportunity—a chance to finally take off the mask and find your way back to your authentic self.

My greatest hope is that as you turn these pages, you will no longer feel isolated. I want you to understand that the silent battles you are fighting are not unique to you. By sharing my story and my truth, I aim to build a bridge from isolation to connection. I want you to walk away feeling seen, understood, and part of a community of women who are ready to let go of the pretense and find true, strength in their shared authenticity.

This book is for all of us who have ever tried to be perfect. Welcome home.

Introduction

Shadows. That's where I lived. Not the fleeting kind that dance with the sun, but the heavy, suffocating kind cast by other people's judgments. They told me I was too dark, not smart enough, a product of the *wrong side of the tracks*. A single mother's child, destined for less. Even though my report card screamed *potential*, my lunch ticket whispered *poverty*. Mom worked double shifts, her hands rough, her love fierce, to give me the outward signs of belonging—the styled hair, the polished nails, the coveted sneakers. But inside, I knew. Those green lunch chips, stamped *Free*, were a brand I couldn't wash off. And the whispers in the hallway? They cut deeper than any insult.

Third grade. That's when the real battle began. The teacher, her eyes cold and dismissive, told me I didn't belong in honors. "Your kind," she implied, "doesn't belong here." My kind. A low-income kid, marked by those damn lunch chips. But Mom, a force of nature, wouldn't have it. She stormed into the principal's office, a whirlwind of righteous fury. And just like that, the path was cleared. But the message was clear: I had to fight harder, claw my way up, just to be seen as equal. Mom's words, a soft, steel-edged promise, echoed in my ears: "Baby girl, trust no one but God." It wasn't a comforting platitude. It was a survival guide.

School became a minefield. Every new classroom, a fresh

round of judgment. Teachers, their eyes skimming my skin, not my grades, would say, "You're in the wrong class." A's and B's stared back at me from my report card, silent witnesses to their ignorance. Mom's voice, a constant drumbeat, "No C's. C's mean a life of seeing your way through." And I knew, with a bone-deep certainty, that I'd rather die fighting than live that way.

So, I made a choice. A dangerous, desperate choice. I asked Mom to lie. To inflate her income on the lunch program application. I wanted to erase the *free lunch* brand, to buy my way into their acceptance. And it worked. A little. The whispers didn't stop, but they shifted. The teachers' gazes held a flicker of something else—maybe respect, maybe just less disdain. But the price? I knew I was playing a dangerous game.

Elementary and middle school? Hell. Pure, unadulterated hell. Every day, a battleground. Me against them. Teachers, peers, administrators—all lined up to tell me who I wasn't. I prayed high school would be different. A sanctuary. A place where I could breathe.

Freshman year arrived like a sunrise after a long, dark night. Teachers who saw *me*, not just the labels pinned to my back. They were passionate, ignited with a fire to nurture every student's potential. For the first time, I wasn't just surviving; I was thriving. Clubs, activities, a life blossoming beyond the suffocating shadows. I felt… light. Unburdened. Like I could finally breathe. But that fragile sense of belonging, that hard-won peace, was a mirage. In my junior and senior years, two English teachers, their words sharp as shards of glass, shattered it all. "Not college material," they sneered. The old familiar sting, the doubt, the fear—it all came flooding back, threatening to drown me.

But I wasn't the same girl they'd tried to crush years before. The scars were there, yes, but they'd woven themselves into a kind of armor. Puberty hadn't just changed my body; it had forged a steel spine. Their words, once razor-sharp, now bounced off me, hollow echoes in a room I'd learned to fill with my own voice. Mom's voice, a constant, unwavering shield, echoed in my heart: *I'm in your corner*. And for the first time, I truly believed it.

Then came the guidance counselor. A woman with eyes that sized me up like a cheap dress, not a student with dreams. "You need to go to the pant factory," she said, her voice flat, dismissive. "Your mom worked there, didn't she?" It wasn't advice. It was a sentence. A life sentence, handed down without a trial.

A red haze of fury clouded my vision. That's when Mom's voice, a whisper of steel, cut through the rage: *Baby girl, depend on God because He is the only one who can see you through.* I wanted to scream, to shatter the room with my anger. Instead, I met her gaze with a glare that could have frozen hell. "Lady," I hissed, "have you lost your mind?"

Graduation. It wasn't just a ceremony; it was a defiant act. A raised fist against every voice that had told me *no*. College, a new battlefield, yes, but this time, I wasn't alone. I found my tribe—first-generation warriors, dreamers forged in the fires of adversity, all of us carrying the weight of our families' hopes. We were a force, a collective *yes* screamed into the face of a world that had tried to silence us. We were the embodiment of "against all odds," a living, breathing testament to the power of resilience. We weren't just seeking a degree; we were carving out a future, not just for ourselves, but for generations to come.

Then, he arrived. Not just a man, but a force. My Boaz. He moved with a quiet confidence that drew me in, a gentle

3

strength that soothed the raw edges of my soul. His eyes, warm and knowing, seemed to see past the scars, past the labels, straight to the woman I was fighting to become. He listened, truly listened, to my dreams, my fears, the stories etched in the lines of my past. He spoke of shared values, of building a life rooted in faith and purpose. He brought me flowers, not just once, but consistently, each bloom a silent promise of his devotion. He called, not with fleeting texts, but with long, thoughtful conversations that stretched into the night. He made me feel seen, cherished, worthy. In a world that had always tried to diminish me, he amplified my voice. He was a balm to my wounded spirit, a beacon of hope in a long, dark night. He was everything I'd ever prayed for, a love story written in the stars. Or so, I desperately believed.

Then, on a night bathed in the soft glow of candlelight, he knelt. Not with rehearsed words, but with a raw vulnerability that laid his soul bare. His eyes, pools of unwavering devotion, locked onto mine. "Will you marry me?" he whispered, his voice thick with emotion. "Will you be my partner, my equal, my forever?" The words, a promise whispered on the breath of angels, felt like a sacred vow. A *yes* erupted from the depths of my being, a joyous explosion of hope and love. In that moment, I wasn't just accepting a proposal; I was accepting a destiny, a future painted in the vibrant colors of our shared dreams.

The embrace that followed was a timeless communion, a silent promise etched in the language of touch. It felt like coming home, like finding the missing piece of my soul. But then, as the euphoria began to settle, the details emerged, like cracks appearing in a flawless facade. Plans made in my absence, a future sculpted without my voice. "We'll move," he announced, his tone casual, almost dismissive. "You'll leave college. Be my wife, my housewife." The words, once a symbol of love, now echoed like a cruel joke. The dream, once so vibrant and alive, shattered into a million pieces, leaving behind a chilling emptiness and a growing, suffocating fear. The man I thought I knew, the man who had promised me a partnership, had revealed himself to be a stranger, a puppeteer pulling strings I didn't even know existed.

The words hung in the air, thick and heavy, like a shroud suffocating the last vestiges of my hope. *Leave college*. The very foundation of my dreams, the promise I made to myself and my family, threatened to crumble. A coldness spread through my veins, a chilling premonition of a life I didn't recognize, a life where my voice was silenced, my aspirations extinguished. The man I thought I loved, the man who had painted a future of shared dreams, was now a stranger, a ghost of the man I'd believed him to be.

The unraveling was swift and brutal. Depression, a dark predator, stalked me in the shadows, whispering insidious lies, stealing the vibrant colors of my world. Twenty pounds heavier, my reflection a distorted stranger, my grades a testament to my crumbling focus—I was losing myself, piece by agonizing piece. The woman I had fought so hard to become, the woman who had dared to dream, was fading, replaced by a hollow shell of despair.

I could not see myself giving up my dreams to become a housewife. I could not give up completing my degree. He could not understand why not. Therefore, my happy *Yes* became sorrowful, *No*, and we drifted apart. I was horrified!

The unraveling wasn't a slow fade; it was a violent storm tearing through the landscape of my soul. Depression, a ravenous beast, clawed at my spirit, whispering lies that echoed the voices of my past: *You're not worthy. You're not enough.* My reflection, once a beacon of strength, now stared back at me with vacant eyes, a stranger bearing the weight of a broken heart.

Yet, even in the suffocating abyss, a tiny, defiant spark refused to be extinguished. My friends, my professors—those warriors who had battled their own demons—became my anchors. Their voices, a lifeline in the raging storm, whispered truths I had forgotten: "You are not defined by this. You are stronger than your pain." They sat with me in the darkness, not offering empty platitudes, but sharing their own scars, their own stories of survival. It wasn't just support; it was a collective act of defiance against the shadows that threatened to consume us all. They showed me that brokenness didn't mean defeat; it meant a deeper understanding of resilience.

The battle was a grueling, internal war, a fight to reclaim my stolen self. To resurrect the woman buried beneath the rubble of shattered dreams, to silence the insidious whispers of self-doubt—it was a Herculean task. I clung to faith, to the melody of a song that echoed the words of my mother, the unwavering belief of my friends. 'His grace and mercy saw me through'—a mantra whispered in the darkest hours, a shield against the onslaught of despair. Each small victory, each step forward, was a testament to the enduring power of the human spirit, a reminder that even in the face of utter devastation, hope could bloom.

"Graduation. Again. Not just a ceremony, but a triumphant resurrection. A declaration of victory against the forces that sought to silence my voice, to extinguish my light. College, a chapter closed, but a new, powerful narrative unfolding. My calling: to be a beacon for others, to illuminate the paths of those lost in the shadows, to prove that even from the depths of despair, we can rise, transformed, and more radiant than ever. To show the world that scars are not signs of weakness, but maps of survival, testaments to the strength forged in the fires of adversity. And so, I stepped into my purpose, into a career where I could make a tangible difference, where my voice could amplify the silenced, my presence a testament to the power of resilience. Success followed, promotions a validation of my dedication, and a deep, abiding gratitude for the path I had walked. God, in His infinite grace, had indeed been good."

1

The Illusion of "Boaz"

The question lingered, a quiet echo in the triumphant silence: *So, now what'* I had conquered academic mountains, scaled professional heights, yet a part of me remained unfulfilled. A yearning for a partner, not defined by my own stringent requirements, but by a divine design. I yearned for a Boaz, a man of valor, a reflection of the biblical figure who embodied kindness, generosity, and unwavering honor. A man who placed Ruth's needs before his own, who possessed a humble spirit yet acted with bold purpose. In my heart, I saw myself as Ruth, the last becoming first, a testament to God's transformative power. I had walked through the shadows, endured the scorn of those who doubted my potential, but God, in His infinite grace, was turning my situation around. Favor, a costly and undeserved gift, had been bestowed upon me. "Look where He brought me from!" the lyrics of Walter Hawkins echoed in my soul, a constant reminder of my journey. I remained humbled, understanding that my time in the back did not diminish my worth, that God's timing was perfect, and that my Boaz would arrive in His appointed season.

The doctorate, a hard-won laurel, a testament to my resilience, became a silent question mark. I had achieved the pinnacle of academic success, yet a quiet ache, a deep-seated longing, resonated within me. The Boaz I had envisioned, the partner who would walk beside me in purpose and faith, remained elusive. Success, I discovered, was a solitary summit if there was no one to share its breathtaking view. The woman who had conquered academic mountains, who had defied every voice that whispered no, now yearned for a different kind of victory: a love story written not in the ink of ambition, but in the sacred language of partnership. I craved a connection that mirrored the strength and grace I'd found within myself, a love that would amplify, not diminish, my light. Little did I know, the very man I believed was my answered prayer, the Boaz I had so earnestly sought, would soon become the architect of my deepest heartbreak, a stark reminder that even the most fervent prayers can be answered in ways we least expect.

He arrived, a figure seemingly sculpted from my deepest desires, a living embodiment of the Boaz I had envisioned. He moved with a quiet authority, a gentle strength that seemed to soothe the lingering wounds of my past. His words, seasoned with wisdom and laced with promises of partnership, resonated with the deepest longings of my soul. He spoke of building a life rooted in faith, of shared purpose, of a love that transcended the ordinary. He saw me, or so I believed, not as a woman defined by her achievements, but as a soul worthy of love, respect, and unwavering devotion. He brought flowers, not as fleeting gestures, but as consistent affirmations of his affection. He called, not with hurried texts, but with long, thoughtful conversations that stretched into the quiet hours of the night. He made me feel seen, cherished, *worthy*. In a world that had

9

often tried to diminish my light, he seemed to amplify it, to celebrate the very essence of who I was. And I, a woman who had learned to trust her own strength, dared to believe that this time, love would be different. This time, I would find a partner who walked beside me, not behind me, a Boaz who would be my equal, my confidant, my sanctuary.

The illusion, however, was a masterfully crafted mirage, a fragile facade that concealed a darker reality. The subtle shifts began as whispers, barely audible at first. The frequency of his calls diminished, the thoughtful conversations replaced by hurried exchanges. The flowers, once a symbol of devotion, became sporadic, almost obligatory. His words, once laced with promises of partnership, now carried a subtle undertone of control, a hint of expectations that didn't align with the shared vision we had painted. I texted, I called, I emailed—a desperate attempt to bridge the growing distance—but he didn't respond. When I finally saw him, I greeted him with a forced smile, a desperate attempt to maintain the illusion. "I've been trying to reach you," I shared, my voice trembling slightly. He looked at me with a chilling detachment, a look that sent a shiver down my spine. "Why are you questioning me?" he retorted, his voice laced with irritation. Now, he accused me of being a nag, of making mountains out of molehills. "I'm busy," he stated, his tone dismissive. "I don't have time for constant calls and texts." I felt compelled to believe him, to cling to the remnants of the Boaz I had envisioned. I loved him, and I didn't want to push him away, to shatter the fragile illusion of our forever. So, I silenced my doubts, buried my instincts, and began to question myself more and more.

The silence became a suffocating shroud, a heavy blanket that smothered my spirit. I withdrew, isolating myself from friends and family, waiting for his calls, his texts, his return to the man I thought I knew. I lost myself in the labyrinth of my own thoughts, desperately trying to decipher the cryptic messages of his silence. I stared at my reflection, a stranger gazing back at me. Fifteen pounds heavier, my once vibrant hair now dull and lifeless, I didn't recognize the woman in the mirror. "Am I a nag?" I whispered, the words echoing the accusations he had hurled. 'What did I do wrong'" The questions gnawed at my soul, eroding my self-worth, chipping away at the foundation of my identity. "Am I no longer his Ruth?" I wondered, the biblical parallel now a cruel irony. "Have I lost my compassion, my devotion, my grace?" The doubts seeped in, a venomous poison that tainted every memory, every shared moment. I clung to my faith, to the belief that God would see me through, that this was merely a test, a trial to strengthen my resolve. I prayed, I listened to worship music, I sought solace in the words of scripture, desperately hoping for a sign, a glimmer of hope. I had chosen my china pattern, a symbol of our future, a testament to my unwavering belief in our forever. And then, he called.

He wanted to talk. A serious talk. After three months of silence, of unanswered calls and ignored texts, I felt a surge of hope, a desperate belief that we could salvage what remained of our shattered dream. "Thank you, God!" I whispered, a prayer of gratitude escaping my lips. He arrived, and my heart fluttered with anticipation. *A serious talk*, I thought, my mind racing with possibilities. Is he going to propose? Is he going to apologize? But the words that followed shattered the fragile hope that had bloomed in my heart.

"I need my space,' he declared, his voice devoid of emotion. "I think the relationship is too serious." Space? Too serious?

The words echoed in the hollow chambers of my heart, a cruel joke played on my deepest desires. "Too serious?" I murmured, my voice barely a whisper. "We've been together for over a year. We've shared dreams, built memories, supported each other." I recounted the moments, the milestones, the promises we had made, but my words fell on deaf ears. "I helped you achieve your short-term goals," I pleaded, "because I loved you, because I believed in us." But my love, my loyalty, my unwavering support—they meant nothing. He had already made his decision. *This is a nightmare*, I thought, my mind reeling. "Someone, please wake me up." He left, leaving behind a trail of shattered illusions and a gaping wound in my soul.

I found myself on the bathroom floor, the cold tiles a stark reminder of my brokenness. Tears streamed down my face, but they felt hollow, empty. I knelt, my body trembling, my spirit crushed. "God, give me strength," I whispered, my voice barely audible. I tried to stand, to pull myself up, but my legs buckled beneath me. I was trapped, not just on the bathroom floor, but in a prison of my own making. "I need a friend," I cried out, my voice raw with pain, a desperate plea for solace in the face of utter devastation.

The bathroom floor, cold and unforgiving, became my sanctuary, a place where I could unravel the tangled threads of my shattered illusions. Tears, hot and bitter, streamed down my face, a release of the pain, the betrayal, the crushing weight of disappointment. How could I, a woman who had conquered so much, find myself broken and humiliated, weeping on a cold, tiled surface? The shame, the embarrassment, the sheer disbelief—it was a tempest raging within me. I had believed, with every fiber of my being, that this time, love would be different. But *love*, I was learning, was not a fairytale, not a guaranteed happily ever after. It was a battlefield, a place where illusions shattered and hearts were laid bare. And in that moment, on that cold, unforgiving floor, I realized that I was not alone. That countless other women, strong, intelligent, and capable, had also found themselves weeping on bathroom floors, victims of broken promises and shattered dreams.

The realization was a turning point, a catalyst for transformation. I saw their faces in my tears, their stories etched in the lines of my despair. Women who, like me, had dared to believe in love, only to find themselves betrayed and abandoned. Women who, like me, had been taught to believe that their strength was a threat, their success a burden. And in that moment, amidst the shattered pieces of my own heart, a new calling emerged: to reach out to those women, to extend a hand from the bathroom floor, to remind them that they were not alone, that their voices mattered, and that their strength could be reclaimed. To show them that even in the midst of heartbreak, they were not broken, but warriors, ready to rise, stronger and more radiant than before.

In the depths of that desolate place, on that cold, unforgiving floor, something shifted within me. The tears, once a symbol of my brokenness, became a baptism, a cleansing of the illusions that had blinded me. The pain, once a crushing weight, became a forge, shaping me into a warrior. I realized that my worth was not defined by his love, or his absence. It was etched in the scars I carried, in the resilience I had cultivated, in the strength I had discovered in the face of utter devastation. I rose, not with anger, not with bitterness, but with a quiet determination. I would not allow his betrayal to define my story. I would not allow his absence to dim my light. I would reclaim my voice, rebuild my shattered dreams, and emerge from the ashes, stronger and more radiant than ever before. The bathroom floor, once a symbol of my defeat, became a launching pad, a place where I found my purpose. And I knew, with a certainty that resonated in the depths of my soul, that I would not only rise, but I would extend a hand to every woman still trapped on her own bathroom floor, and together, we would rewrite our stories, not as victims, but as victors.

2

Get Naked

There comes a reckoning in every life, a moment when the soul demands to be laid bare. Not physically, though the vulnerability is just as profound. Figuratively, it's a stripping away of the carefully constructed façade, a shedding of the armor we wear to face the world. It's the desperate need to confide, to unravel the tangled threads of our truth before a witness, someone who will listen without judgment, who will hold our shattered pieces with tenderness and allow us to walk away with our dignity intact. I craved that intimacy, that raw, unfiltered connection. I yearned for a sanctuary where I could lay my burdens down, where my voice wouldn't be met with platitudes or dismissive sighs. But there was no sanctuary, no confidant, no safe harbor. Instead, I found myself, literally naked, sprawled face down on the cold bathroom tiles, my body a testament to the utter depletion of my spirit. The man I thought was my Boaz, the man I now knew as Terry, had vanished.

There was no escape, no alternative. Silence was my only companion, the heavy, suffocating kind that amplified the echoes of my own despair. There was no one to hear the story of Terry, the man who had promised me forever, only to demand space when forever was within reach. The china pattern, a symbol of our shared future, now mocked me with its empty promise. The venue, chosen with dreams of celebration, now loomed as a monument to my shattered illusions. For almost a year, we had built a world of us, a world that now lay in ruins. Why did this happen? How could I face the world, my family, my friends, myself? And the questions, like vultures circling a wounded animal, would begin their relentless assault this morning, in the unforgiving glare of the church pews.

Help me, God! The tears were a relentless torrent, a flood threatening to drown me in my own shame. I was mortified. Terry and I, a fixture at church every Sunday. Me, in the choir, my voice raised in praise. Him, a welcoming smile at the door, a greeter. Now, the thought of facing those familiar faces, the inevitable questions, the unspoken judgments—it was unbearable. Oh God, what would they say? What could I possibly say? Could I even summon the strength to walk through those doors? Was I ready to expose the raw, bleeding wound of my heartbreak to the world?

I knew, intellectually, that I needed to rise, to prepare for the inevitable ordeal of church. But my body refused to obey. I remained sprawled on the cold, unforgiving tiles, a broken doll abandoned on the floor. My sobs, once a desperate plea for solace, now echoed like a hollow lament. I was empty, devoid of strength, a shell of the woman I once was. With my face pressed against the cold, hard surface, my tears blurring my vision, I noticed the intricate patterns of the tiles—the subtle variations in color, the delicate veins running through the stone. Ten years I had lived in this house, but only now, in this moment of utter despair, did I truly *see* them. I had never been so intimately acquainted with my bathroom floor. How could I possibly find the strength to stand? Each desperate attempt to rise ended in failure, my body collapsing against the rim of the toilet, a testament to my utter helplessness.

The night bled into morning, the cold tiles my only comfort. Seven a.m., the phone's shrill ring cut through the silence, a cruel reminder of Sunday's routine. My stomach clenched, a wave of nausea washing over me. Terry's Sunday call, the familiar ritual, now a phantom echo of what was lost. I lunged for the phone on my nightstand, a desperate hope flickering in my chest. Maybe…just maybe… But it wasn't Terry. It was the choir director, a cheerful voice detailing the morning's attire. The color to wear, a detail that now felt like a cruel mockery of my shattered world.

The bile rose in my throat, a bitter taste of disappointment. It wasn't him. I stumbled back to the bathroom, the tiles now familiar companions in my despair, and the tears erupted, a fresh wave of grief washing over me. "Help me, God!" I choked out, my voice a ragged whisper. How could I face this day? How could I face them?

Summoning a strength, I didn't know I possessed, I forced myself into the shower, the hot water a futile attempt to wash away the stain of my heartbreak. But the tears continued, an unstoppable flood, a testament to the depths of my pain. "Where are they coming from?" I whispered, the question a hollow echo in the steam-filled room. I had to go to church. I repeated the mantra like a desperate prayer, a plea for the strength to face the day. Slowly, painstakingly, I dressed, each movement a Herculean task. It felt like an eternity before I finally stood, a fragile facade of composure. Appearances. That was the currency of survival. I had to pull myself together, to construct a mask of normalcy, a charade that would conceal the raw, bleeding wound beneath. No one could know the truth, the humiliating reality of my night spent on the bathroom floor. As I drove towards the church, the weight of my isolation settled upon me, a suffocating blanket of loneliness. I was alone, utterly alone, and I would have to face them all, their curious eyes, their inevitable questions about Terry's absence. The emotions threatened to overwhelm me, to shatter the fragile composure I had so painstakingly assembled. But I knew I couldn't break. I had to fake it. I had to perform happiness, a joy that was nowhere to be found, a lie that would hopefully keep the vultures at bay.

The car door slammed, a resounding echo in the quiet morning, and I faced the daunting expanse of the church's entrance. The walk, normally a casual stroll, now stretched before me like an endless gauntlet. Would Terry be there, a greeter at the door, a cruel twist of fate? I was a carefully constructed illusion, a masterpiece of outward composure. My choir attire, meticulously chosen, clung to my frame like armor. My hair, a perfect cascade of curls, framed a face painted with flawless precision. My lipstick, a defiant crimson, masked the trembling of my lips. No one, I told myself, would see the storm raging within. This was not the time or place for raw vulnerability, for the messy, naked truth. I was a fortress, a bastion of strength, and I would not crumble. But with each step, the fortress weakened, the bastion faltered. My stomach churned, a knot of anxiety tightening with every breath. "'Hold it together," I whispered, a desperate mantra against the rising tide of panic. "You're almost there." But the lie was a fragile shield, and I knew, with a bone-deep certainty, that I was about

18

to break. I was going to be sick, right here, right now, in front of everyone.

The heavy church doors swung open, and the two greeters, their smiles wide and welcoming, greeted me in perfect unison. "Good morning! Where's Terry?" The question, sharp and unexpected, sliced through the fragile composure I had so painstakingly constructed. It was a casual inquiry, a simple greeting, but it landed like a physical blow, a stark reminder of the absence I was desperately trying to conceal.

The words hung in the air, a suffocating cloud of unspoken questions. My stomach lurched, a wave of nausea threatening to betray the carefully constructed facade. *Oh my*, I thought, the panic rising in my throat, if I speak, I will be sick. I forced a smile, a brittle mask that threatened to crack at any moment. "Good morning," I replied, my voice light and airy, a performance of normalcy. "Hopefully, Terry is on his way!" The lie, so casually spoken, felt like a lead weight in my mouth, a heavy burden added to the already unbearable weight of my grief

The sanctuary doors swung shut behind me, sealing me in a space that now felt like a battleground. And there she was, the self-appointed guardian of church gossip, the Mother of the Church, her eyes sharp and probing. "Good morning, sister!" she chirped, her voice laced with thinly veiled curiosity. "Where's Terry?" The question, delivered with the practiced ease of a seasoned interrogator, landed like a sharp, unexpected blow. It wasn't a casual inquiry; it was a demand for information, a subtle accusation wrapped in a veneer of concern

The biting retort, *He's not in my pocket*, simmered just beneath the surface, a venomous whisper I dared not unleash. Instead, I offered a strained smile, a brittle mask of polite indifference, and retreated to my place in the choir stand. From my vantage point, I could scan the congregation, a silent vigil for Terry's arrival. Each passing moment, each empty pew, fueled a conflicting mix of anxiety and relief. I longed to know he was okay, to send a text, a lifeline in the silent void between us. But his words, "I need space," echoed in my mind, a cold reminder of the chasm that now separated us. A part of me, weary and wounded, was grateful for his absence, for the reprieve from the inevitable confrontation. Just getting here, to this sanctuary of forced smiles and carefully constructed lies, had been a Herculean task. I wasn't ready to face him, not yet, perhaps not ever.

The final hymn faded, a bittersweet release, and I launched my escape, a strategic retreat towards the sanctuary doors. Every polite nod, every forced smile, was a hurdle I had to overcome. But my carefully orchestrated exit was thwarted. Just as my hand touched the cool metal of the door handle, Deacon Stephens, a man whose voice boomed like a biblical prophet, intercepted me.

His voice, a booming echo in the emptying sanctuary, cut through my last vestiges of composure. "Where's Terry, sister? We truly missed him today. Please let him know he was missed today," he rattled off, the words a rapid-fire barrage of unwanted attention. My smile, now a strained grimace, faltered. "Yes, Deacon Stephens, I'll do just that," I managed, my voice tight, as I quickened my pace towards the sanctuary doors, towards the sanctuary of my car.

But he wasn't finished. "Why are you in such a hurry, sister" he asked, his voice laced with a thinly veiled curiosity that felt like a violation. My patience, already stretched to its breaking point, snapped. "I simply have a lot to do today, and I'm trying to get to my next appointment," I replied, my voice clipped, each word a carefully measured attempt to conceal the rising tide of anger and despair.

"God, please forgive me for that lie," I whispered under my breath, the words a silent plea for absolution. The guilt, a sharp, piercing pain, added another layer to the already unbearable weight of my grief. Even in my desperation, I couldn't escape the sting of dishonesty, the knowledge that I had compromised my own integrity in a moment of weakness.

Finally, the sanctuary doors were behind me, and I collapsed into the sanctuary of my car, the tears threatening to spill over. The drive home, normally a familiar comfort, felt like an endless journey through a desolate landscape. What was I supposed to do with the rest of this empty day? Terry, my Terry, was supposed to be here. We were supposed to be having brunch, laughing, living. But he wasn't. The radio, a cruel twist of fate, began to play "I Believe" by James Fortune and FIYA, the powerful melody and lyrics a stark contrast to the despair that threatened to consume me. The dam broke, and the tears flowed, a torrent of grief blurring my vision. " believe, I believe, I believe," I whispered, the words a desperate mantra against the rising tide of hopelessness. Each mile felt like an eternity, each passing street a reminder of the life I had lost. I finally reached my doorstep, a threshold I could barely cross. My legs buckled, and I crumpled to my knees, a broken figure on the cold concrete. With a final, desperate surge of energy, I crawled to the nearest chair, a refuge in my desolate home, and cried out, my voice raw with anguish, "Why me? Why me?"

The questions swirled, a relentless vortex of self-blame. "What happened? What did I do wrong?" My mind, once a fortress of confidence, now echoed with the insidious whispers of doubt. I scrutinized my reflection, finding flaws where none existed, fixating on my weight, my appearance, the very essence of my being. I became a prisoner of my own insecurities, trapped in a cycle of self-deprecation. Desperate for solace, I turned to prayer, pleading for a sign, a divine intervention to alleviate the crushing weight of guilt. But the silence from above only amplified the hollowness within. I was spiraling, lost in a labyrinth of my own making. Fear, a cold, constricting hand, gripped my heart, isolating me from the very people who could offer comfort. I couldn't bear the thought of my girlfriend's judgment, her well-meaning attempts to understand a pain that felt incomprehensible. And so, I retreated, seeking refuge in the familiar, unforgiving embrace of the bathroom floor, the cold tiles a silent witness to my unraveling. It was there, amidst the shattered fragments of my self-worth, that I finally succumbed to exhaustion, sleep a temporary escape from the relentless torment of my thoughts.

Monday morning. The very phrase felt like a cruel sentence. I had to face them again, the well-meaning colleagues, the casual inquiries that would cut like shards of glass. I could already hear the inevitable chorus: "'How was your weekend? What did you and Terry do?" I had been trained, conditioned, to compartmentalize, to leave the messy wreckage of my personal life at the door. And so, I donned my mask, a carefully crafted facade of normalcy. I plastered on a smile, a counterfeit beacon of cheer, and greeted my co-workers with a forced "Happy Monday." I navigated the office, a minefield of potential questions, desperately trying to avoid the inevitable "weekend" query.

But my efforts were futile. The question, like a persistent mosquito, found its way to my ear. "How was your weekend?"

they asked, their tone light, oblivious to the storm raging within. I offered a clipped, "I stayed home," a bare-bones answer designed to shut down further conversation. Please, just let me reach my office, my sanctuary, my temporary escape. I sank into my chair, the cool leather a small comfort, and took a deep, shuddering breath. Then, my phone vibrated, a jolt of anxiety electrifying my nerves. My stomach clenched, a knot of dread tightening with each pulse. Was it him? Could it be? I glanced at the screen, and my heart sank. It was my mother, her voice a cheerful melody I had no strength to endure. "What's wrong?" she asks, her tone laced with concern, a question I didn't have the energy to answer.

Calmly, I say, "I am working."

Mom finally hangs up the phone, and I take another deep breath. This is going to be a long day. I find myself working late hours. I didn't want to go home. I hated the weekends; I didn't have anything to do anymore. I find myself just existing. The glow of the monitor was a cold comfort, a stark contrast to the emptiness that awaited me in my apartment. Each line of code, each carefully constructed sentence, was a barrier, a shield against the silence. I'd become a master of distractions, a virtuoso of late-night deadlines. The office, with its hum of servers and the distant clatter of the cleaning crew, was my sanctuary. Here, I could lose myself in the minutiae, postpone the inevitable confrontation with the hollow space I called home.

Terry has missed two consecutive Sundays. What is really going on? I want to call, so I text and I don't get a response and that sets me even farther back. I will never get off the bathroom floor.

It was a bright, crisp Monday morning, the kind that usually held the promise of a fresh start. I walked into the office, forcing a wide, cheerful smile, "Happy Monday!" I announced, but the team, gathered in a tight huddle, looked at me with a mixture of concern and confusion. *Why is she so happy?* their eyes seemed to ask. I retreated to my office, the forced cheerfulness already beginning to fray, and buried myself in work, trying to recapture the illusion of control. The hours ticked by, a relentless march towards lunch, when a co-worker came to my door, her expression hesitant. "Are you alright?" she asked, and I managed a strained, "Sure, what's up?" She asked if she could sit, and I nodded, a knot of dread tightening in my stomach. Then, she delivered the blow: a co-worker saw Terry with another woman.

The carefully constructed walls I'd built around myself began to crack. *I'm going to die*, the thought echoed in my mind, a frantic, silent scream. I wanted to expel her from my office, to erase the words she'd spoken. Instead, I tried to maintain the illusion, the fragile pretense of composure. "That's… that's impossible," I stammered, "She must be mistaken. That was his cousin." The co-worker's smirk was a physical blow, a confirmation of my deepest fears. The late hours, the relentless work, the forced cheerfulness – all of it was a lie, a desperate attempt to outrun the pain. Now, the lie was crumbling, revealing the raw, exposed nerves beneath. The office, my sanctuary, suddenly felt like a trap, the walls closing in. The smile I'd pasted on my face felt like a grotesque mask, a mockery of my true feelings. I wanted to shatter something, to scream until my voice was raw, but I simply sat there, a hollow shell, as the world around me began to spin.

I wanted to run out of the office, take an extended lunch break, and just hide. When I finally left for lunch, it felt like everyone was watching, their eyes burning into my back. I drove as fast as possible to my house, a desperate need to escape the suffocating atmosphere. When I slammed the door behind me, I hollered, a raw, animalistic cry that echoed through the empty rooms, probably scaring the neighbor half to death. I knew I couldn't stay away for long, couldn't give them the satisfaction of seeing me break. I forced myself to return, to adhere to the rigid structure of the workday, even as my world was falling apart. I walked back into the office, head held high, and made a conscious effort to engage with my co-workers, to pretend that everything was normal. Inside, I was dying, a slow, agonizing death. *Help me, Holy Ghost!* I silently pleaded, a desperate prayer in the face of overwhelming pain.

I go back to my office and turn on the radio. "I Believe" comes on, and the dam breaks again. I begin to sob, but this time, it's a quiet, desperate weeping. The lyrics, a promise that "the storm will soon be over," are a cruel irony, a fleeting hope that feels impossibly distant. I retreat to the bathroom, seeking a moment of solitude, a chance to gather my strength, to pray for resilience. But instead, I feel myself weakening, the weight of the day pressing down on me, crushing my spirit. Each breath is a struggle, each prayer a faint whisper in the face of the overwhelming despair.

What am I going to do? The week is almost over, praise God. I decide to try and reinvent myself, believing that a new look might somehow mend the cracks in my heart. I purchased the most expensive Brazilian hair, went on a whirlwind shopping spree, and returned home, hoping for a transformation. But as soon as I opened the door, the carefully constructed facade shattered like glass. I crumpled to the floor, the weight of my unchanged reality a crushing blow. The new hair, the expensive clothes – they were just costumes, flimsy disguises for the raw, gaping wound inside. I had a new look, but the same broken heart, the same agonizing silence.

Terry was gone, a month of absence stretching into an unbearable eternity. It was time for church, another Sunday, another forced march towards a place that offered no solace. Each step towards the door was a battle, a heavy, agonizing trek. I knew what awaited me: the relentless questions, the prying eyes, the silent judgment of the sisters, each glance a sharp, invisible knife twisting in the wound. The performance was about to begin, and I was the lead actress in a tragedy I couldn't escape.

I have my new hair, my new outfit, my face beat, and my red lipstick. The greeters open the door, and the world stops. Terry. He's standing there, a solid, impossible figure at the threshold. It's like a physical blow. My breath catches, a strangled gasp in my throat. My heart doesn't just drop; it plummets, a stone falling into a dark, bottomless well. *I am going to be sick; I am going to be sick*, a silent scream echoes in my head, a frantic, desperate plea. The carefully crafted image – the hair, the clothes, the bold red lipstick – dissolves into nothingness, a fragile facade exposed.

My legs tremble, threatening to give way. The sounds of the church, the murmuring greetings, fade into a distant, distorted hum. All my senses narrow, focusing on him. It's like a dream, a nightmare, a cruel hallucination. He's here, and every ounce of my carefully constructed composure is shattering into a million pieces. The air is thick, suffocating, and I'm trapped, a deer caught in the headlights, unable to move, unable to breathe.

I talk to myself… "You look good, so smile."

But I can't. My face feels like it's made of fragile glass, ready to shatter. Terry speaks with such infuriating confidence, like nothing is wrong. A surge of rage, hot and sharp, rises in me. I want to punch him, to wipe that smug look off his face. "Why are you speaking to me, when you didn't even answer my texts?" I manage, my voice tight. "It's okay," I force out, trying to reclaim some semblance of control, "because I'm looking fabulous today."

The praise and worship team is on fire, the music a soaring wave of emotion. The spirit in the room is high, almost feverish. And then, the Pastor begins to preach. His text: "The Storm Is Almost Over." The words hit me like a physical force. My spirit, already a chaotic mix of anger and pain, begins to stir, a flicker of hope battling with the raw hurt. I try to stay calm, to maintain the facade, but my legs are shaking, a physical manifestation of the turmoil within. "Preach, Pastor, preach," I whisper, a desperate plea for something, anything, to break through the walls I've built around myself.

The Pastor's words ignite something within me, a fire that spreads through my veins. I begin to speak, a torrent of words in my heavenly language, a raw, untamed expression of the storm raging within. The world around me blurs, the music swells, and then, a sudden stillness. A sheet is draped across me, a tangible manifestation of the Holy Spirit's presence, a moment of surrender and release. The intensity of the experience leaves me shaken, vulnerable.

After the service, I'm a whirlwind of motion, desperate to escape. I practically run to my car, needing to put distance between myself and the lingering intensity of the moment, and the inevitable confrontation with Terry. I knew he'd try to talk to me, to maintain the illusion of our relationship, to keep up appearances for the congregation. I scan the parking lot, my heart pounding, and then, a wave of disappointment washes over me. His car is gone. He's already left, abandoning me to the aftermath, to the questions I didn't want to answer.

Really... he doesn't want to talk to me. The thought hits me like a slap, a stinging betrayal. A torrent of questions floods my mind, each one a jagged shard of pain. "Who is this woman he's seeing?" "What are they doing?" "Oh my God, he looked so good today." The lingering scent of his cologne, a cruel reminder of intimacy, fills my senses, making me want to scream. *Get it together,* I command myself, the words a desperate mantra against the rising tide of panic.

I spot his car at the traffic light, a fleeting glimpse of the man who's tearing me apart. In a desperate whisper, I plead with myself, "Don't panic!" The light changes, and he disappears, leaving me alone with the wreckage of my emotions. I drive home, a numb, mechanical process, and the moment I cross the threshold, the carefully constructed walls crumble. I collapse onto the bathroom floor, the cool tiles a stark contrast to the burning rage and grief consuming me.

The phone rings, a jarring intrusion into my solitude. My girlfriend's voice, usually a source of comfort, is sharp with concern. "What is going on with you? Who are you? Why are you avoiding me? I know your love life is not *that* heavy!"

Why did she have to say that? The casual dismissal, the assumption that my pain was somehow trivial, was the final straw. A raw, guttural cry erupts from my chest, a sound of pure, unadulterated pain. "Terry and I are not together anymore," I sob, the words a broken confession. "I don't know what to do." The dam breaks, and the tears flow, a torrent of grief and confusion. I can't stop crying, the sobs racking my body, each one a release of the agony I've been holding inside.

My friend didn't hang up the phone. Instead, she drove straight to my house, and we cried together, a shared release of pain. In her presence, I felt a profound sense of safety, a space where I could finally shed the layers of pretense and expose the raw, bleeding wound of my heart. I was able to get naked with her, not physically, but emotionally, laying bare my most intimate thoughts, the deepest fears and desires I had kept hidden. I wasn't ashamed to share the details of what had happened, the agonizing confusion of Terry's betrayal, the depth of my love for him, a love that now felt like a cruel, jagged scar. I thank God for her, for the unwavering support she offered. I could call her at any hour, day or night, and she would answer, her voice a constant lifeline in the midst of my despair. For some strange, inexplicable reason, she was always there, always ready to listen.

One evening, I was out driving, and I saw Terry. He was in his car, with another woman. He didn't see me. A war erupted within me. My left brain screamed, *Follow them! Find out where they're going!* My right brain whispered, *Go home. Walk away. Protect yourself.* I grabbed my phone, my hand shaking, and called my girlfriend. The words tumbled out of me, a torrent of rage and hurt. I was hollering, calling Terry every name I could think of, a raw, primal scream of pain. I pulled over, my hands gripping the steering wheel, and forced myself to breathe. I counted to ten, trying to regain some semblance of control, to anchor myself in the swirling chaos of my emotions.

My girlfriend wanted to pray. I couldn't. I didn't want her to. Prayer was the last thing on my mind. My veins throbbed with a primal rage. I wanted to follow that car, to rip him out of it, to confront him with the raw, incandescent fury that burned within me. Prayer felt like a betrayal, a surrender I wasn't willing to make. My color started to change, a flush of anger spreading across my skin. *How can anyone pray at a time such as this?* I thought, the question a silent scream of defiance.

I finally made it home, the drive a blur of white-hot rage and desperate self-control. The moment I crossed the threshold, I collapsed onto the floor, the tiles cold against my burning skin. I sobbed for hours, a raw, animalistic sound of grief and betrayal. "So, this is why he needed space," I whispered, the words a bitter, broken revelation. "He was seeing someone else."

It's an extraordinary, almost miraculous thing, to have a friend who sees the madness swirling within you, who witnesses the raw, unraveling edges of your sanity, and yet, still believes in your inherent worth when you've lost all faith in yourself. The phone calls to my friend became a constant lifeline, a desperate plea for sanity in the midst of the storm. The crying spells, once sporadic, became a relentless, daily ritual, a purging of the pain that threatened to consume me.

"What is wrong with me?" I'd scream into the phone, the question a raw, guttural cry. "Why can't I get it together?" The hair and nail salon became a weekly pilgrimage, a desperate attempt to construct a facade of normalcy, a shield against the world's prying eyes. I craved attention, a desperate need to be seen, yet I simultaneously wanted to vanish, to become invisible. I wanted the world to see a strong, composed woman, while only my friend knew the shattered pieces I was desperately trying to glue back together. So, I became someone else, a carefully constructed illusion, a mask I wore to navigate a world that felt both hostile and indifferent. And as I donned this new persona, I knew, with a chilling certainty, that this was just the beginning. The next chapter, I sensed, would demand a level of nakedness I hadn't yet dared to confront.

3

A Nightmare

T he world twisted and contorted, a grotesque carnival of distorted faces and suffocating shadows. I clawed at the air, desperate to escape the suffocating grip of this waking nightmare, but my limbs felt heavy, leaden. I didn't recognize myself, a stranger trapped in a funhouse mirror reflection of my former life. The mask I'd so carefully crafted, a shield against the pain, had become a suffocating cage, trapping me in a performance I couldn't escape. *Wake up,* I screamed inwardly, but the silent plea echoed in the empty chambers of my mind. Why was this happening? I, who paid my tithes, sowed seeds, interceded for the sick and shut-in? I hurled God's own words back at him, a desperate, defiant prayer: "Delight yourself in the Lord and he will give you the desires of your heart." *My heart is broken, God!* I sobbed, the tears burning tracks down my face. *I have been faithful.* And yet, here I was, trapped in this grotesque parody of existence, a Thursday evening reminder that I had choir practice, a place where all would see the lie I was living.

My legs moved on autopilot, carrying me to the church,

where I pasted on the widest, most brittle smile and chirped, "Happy Thursday!" The response was a hollow echo, save for the huddled altos, who turned to me with the vacant, knowing stares of the damned.

My mind was a battlefield, a chaotic clash of suspicion and denial. *They're talking about me,* a voice hissed, sharp and insistent. *No, they wouldn't dare,* I countered, clinging to the last vestiges of sanity. The choir director's request for prayer felt like a carefully orchestrated attack. When the lead singer began to speak, his words were a barbed wire noose tightening around my throat. "Bless the women in the choir who are in denial of their mate cheating on them." The words hung in the air, a neon sign flashing my darkest fears. I felt the blood drain from my face, a cold dread creeping up my spine. *This cannot be happening.* The altos, those self-righteous vultures, became a chorus of "Amens," their voices dripping with sanctimonious glee. *They're enjoying this,* I thought, a surge of raw, animalistic rage bubbling beneath the surface. My faith, once a solid foundation, now felt like a crumbling ruin, each prayer a betrayal.

I knew what I heard. The lead singer's "prayer" was a direct, calculated attack, a thinly veiled accusation that resonated with the deepest, most terrifying truths I was trying to deny. When he finished, I forced a tight smile, "You said your prayers today," I said, the words dripping with a venom I barely recognized. He made me sick, his pious pronouncements a grotesque parody of his own hidden sins. *"No weapon formed against me shall prosper,"* I thought, the phrase a desperate, hollow mantra against the rising tide of rage. He couldn't talk, not with his wife's second child being fathered by Deacon Hilson. *They don't think anyone knows,* I thought, a dark, twisted satisfaction creeping into my anger. *Please don't let me bust you out.* The thoughts swirled in my head, a toxic brew of resentment and the desperate need to reclaim some semblance of control.

I couldn't wait to escape. The suffocating atmosphere of judgment, the knowing glances, the thinly veiled accusations – it was all too much. I should have stayed home, I thought, the realization a bitter, heavy weight. But it is no way I will give them the satisfaction. I wouldn't let them kill my spirit, I told myself, a desperate mantra against the rising tide of despair. The battle within me raged on, a brutal, exhausting war against the encroaching darkness. Sanity felt like a fragile thread, threatening to snap under the relentless pressure. The isolation was a suffocating blanket, smothering me, leaving me gasping for air. I was alone, utterly and completely alone, trapped in a nightmare of my own making, and I had no idea how to wake up.

Finally, I reached my car, my sanctuary on wheels, and I erupted. A raw, guttural scream tore from my throat, a primal release of the pain I had held captive all day. The tears, a deluge now, streamed down my face, blurring my vision until the road disappeared beneath a watery haze. I was blind, lost in a storm of my own making. I pulled over, the engine idling, a trembling beast in the quiet street. I wanted to call someone, anyone, but the thought of well-meaning platitudes, of forced prayers, made my skin crawl. I didn't want comfort; I wanted vengeance. I wanted to inflict the same pain I felt, to make someone, anyone, understand the depth of my suffering. I began to frantically turn the radio dial, seeking a soundtrack for my rage. And then, I heard it. A woman's voice, raw and defiant, cutting through the static: "There's a special place in hell for you." Mary J. Blige. "You gon' pay for what you did to me." The words, a venomous balm to my wounded soul, pierced the fog of my despair. I wiped my tears, my posture straightening, a flicker of something akin to strength igniting within me. I needed to hear this song, from the beginning, to absorb every word, every note of righteous fury. I pulled back onto the road, the music my guide, my battle cry. I made it home, a sanctuary of solitude, and promptly collapsed at the door, the familiar cold of the floor beckoning. I crawled, a broken animal seeking shelter, to the bathroom, my refuge, my confessional, my silent witness to my unraveling.

The bathroom floor, my familiar companion, welcomed me back. I lay there, motionless, a broken vessel emptied of all strength. My mind, a chaotic whirlwind of self-recrimination, spiraled into madness. How had I allowed myself to descend to this abyss? The phone rang, a persistent, jarring intrusion, but it was a distant echo, a sound I couldn't, wouldn't, reach. The only sound that truly resonated was the haunting refrain in my head: "There's a special place in hell for you." I tried to rise, to grasp the porcelain rim of the toilet, but my body betrayed me, collapsing onto the cold tiles. The words, a venomous mantra, repeated in my mind, a constant, cruel echo.

Time blurred, and the relentless knocking at the door jolted me awake. I looked up, disoriented, still sprawled on the bathroom floor. A voice, familiar and concerned, called my name. "Yes?" I managed, my voice hoarse and weak. It was her, my friend, a lifeline in the darkness. "Are you alright" she asked, her voice laced with worry. "Yes," I lied, the word a hollow echo. Summoning a strength, I didn't know I possessed, I dragged myself to the door. She pulled me into her arms, and the dam broke. Another wave of grief, raw and uninhibited, washed over me. I pleaded with God for strength, for the ability to endure this unbearable pain.

She didn't speak, didn't offer platitudes or empty reassurances. She simply held me, allowing me to be naked, to expose the raw, bleeding wound of my heartbreak. She knew, perhaps better than anyone, the depth of my love for Terry, the shattered dreams that now lay in ruins. I poured out my story, the humiliation at church, the cruel questions, the final, devastating confrontation. I told her about the choir practice, the gossip, the betrayal. She listened, her silence a comforting presence in the midst of my storm. She was not surprised about the choir director. "They're all messy," I said, my voice thick with bitterness. "They all have skeletons in their closets. How would they handle a crisis as such as this?"

This raw, gaping wound of betrayal, this crushing weight of loneliness? I felt utterly defeated, a broken soldier on a battlefield of my own making. My phone, a constant reminder of my isolation, displayed 23 missed calls from my friend. The first thing that surfaced in my mind was Psalms 23, a desperate plea for comfort: "The Lord is my shepherd; I shall not want. He maketh me to lie down in green pastures: He leadeth me beside the still waters." What significance did it hold now, in the cold, desolate hours of 3:00 AM, when I had to be at work at 7:00 AM? I begged my friend to stay, desperate for human contact, for a shield against the encroaching darkness. We talked, we cried, we laughed, a fragile attempt to stitch together the shattered pieces of my reality, until the first rays of dawn painted the sky.

The thought of facing them, my co-workers, was a looming dread, a suffocating weight that threatened to crush me. How could I possibly summon the strength to perform normalcy, to plaster on a smile and engage in their casual banter? I was a hollow shell, drained of all vitality, in no mood for their oblivious pleasantries. But there was no escape. I couldn't afford a day off, couldn't bear the thought of them whispering about my inability to cope, to function. It was Friday, a fragile promise of respite, a beacon of hope in the encroaching darkness. "I can make it through today," I whispered, a desperate prayer for strength. I walked into the office, and the receptionist's wide, unsettling smile sent a shiver down my spine. *What does she know?* I thought, my paranoia spiking. *Today is not the day*. I rushed to my office, a sanctuary of sorts, and slammed the door, seeking a moment of respite from the relentless social pressure.

A wave of bone-deep weariness washed over me, a desperate longing for oblivion. I could have succumbed to sleep, a deep, dreamless slumber, a temporary escape from the relentless ache in my soul. But I was trapped, tethered to my desk, a prisoner of my professional obligations. The jarring ring of my phone, followed by a knock at the door, shattered my fragile attempt at focus. "Meeting in ten minutes," a voice announced, a cruel reminder of the demands of the day. "'God, thank you,'" I muttered, the forced distraction a welcome reprieve from the swirling vortex of my thoughts. I would bury myself in work, summon every last ounce of my professional persona, and ignore the lingering bitterness of the choir practice, the gnawing ache of sleeplessness. I looked up at the clock, my stomach twisting with a pang of guilt. Lunchtime had vanished, a forgotten casualty of my self-imposed isolation. *Great*, I thought, 'an hour less of this.' I would leave early, a small victory in a day of defeat.

As I prepared to leave, the receptionist appeared at my door, her cheerful inquiry about my weekend plans a cruel reminder of the life I was missing. I offered a vague, "Resting, me time," a fragile attempt to maintain my composure. Her response, a casual chuckle and a boastful tale of her fabulous weekend, sent a wave of resentment through me. "Get out of my office, you trouble maker" I seethed silently, my smile a thin, brittle mask. Finally, the clock struck five, and I escaped, a fugitive fleeing a prison. But the guilt gnawed at me as I realized I hadn't called my friend, hadn't checked on her, my own pain consuming all my attention. A wave of surprise washed over me as I looked at my phone and saw three missed calls from her. She, who had held me as I fell apart, who had allowed me to be raw and vulnerable, had reached out. I had ignored her. I needed to do something special for her, to acknowledge the depth of her compassion, to repay the kindness of the only person who could truly navigate the labyrinth of my craziness. Perhaps I could treat my friend to a spa day tomorrow? A gesture of gratitude, a way to repay her unwavering support. Yes, that could be a sanctuary, a shared space of healing and renewal. Or maybe, she simply needed a break from my relentless storm of emotions.

I hesitated, then dialed her number, the familiar ring a fragile thread of connection. By the time I reached my car, the weight of exhaustion descended, a physical manifestation of my emotional depletion. I yearned for nothing but sleep, a temporary oblivion. I made it home, a sanctuary turned prison, and collapsed onto the sofa, my body a battleground of conflicting sensations. I drifted in and out of consciousness, my mind a swirling vortex of fragmented thoughts. When I finally surfaced, the clock read 9:00 PM. I called my friend, my voice hoarse and weary. I confessed my dread of facing church on Sunday, the performative smiles and hollow platitudes of those who claimed to cherish the work I do in the ministry. I suggested the spa, a desperate attempt to find solace in shared tranquility. She declined, her voice gentle but firm. "You need rest," she said, a simple truth I couldn't deny. But what was rest? A foreign concept in my current reality.

I knew I had to visit the hair salon, a necessary ritual of preparation for Sunday's service. The thought filled me with dread. The salon, a breeding ground for gossip, a place where secrets were traded like currency. My stylist, her eyes gleaming with morbid curiosity, wasted no time. She recounted, with unnerving detail, Terry's public display of affection with another woman, a patron of the same salon, a different day. "They seemed happy," she chirped, her tone laced with a perverse satisfaction. Why was she telling me this? I wanted to scream, to demand she finish my hair and release me from this torture. I wanted to know every detail, every cruel, insignificant detail, but I held my tongue, refusing to give her the satisfaction of my pain. How long did it take to style someone's hair? Finally, I escaped, a fugitive from the salon's suffocating atmosphere.

As soon as I entered my car, Mary J.'s voice filled the space, the same song, the same venomous lyrics. "There's a special place in hell for you; you gon' pay for what you did to me; I'ma tell you 'cause the truth will see me free, oh." The words, once a source of catharsis, now ignited a firestorm of rage within me. I called my friend, my voice trembling with fury, and recounted the stylist's tale. Her silence, a heavy, unspoken acknowledgment of my pain, fueled my anger.

"How could he?" I cried, my voice raw with betrayal. "Why would he do this? How could he move on so quickly?" I felt myself unraveling, losing control, allowing him to dictate my emotional state. "God," I whispered, my voice thick with despair, "how can you let me endure this?" I reached my home, my sanctuary turned battleground, and collapsed onto the bathroom floor, the cold tiles a familiar comfort. My tears, a relentless torrent, blurred my vision, obscuring the familiar grains in the tile. I couldn't comprehend how I was still so consumed by him. Even as I prayed, even as I served, even as I tithed, I was lost, adrift in a sea of emotional chaos. A psychology degree, a facade of knowledge, was useless against the raw, visceral pain of a broken heart. Life had to improve. I could not continue to exist in this state.

Sunday. The day of supposed sanctuary, now a battleground. I loathed the thought of facing them, the "messy church people," their well-meaning inquiries laced with judgment, their platitudes a thin veil over their curiosity. I would arrive early, a strategic maneuver to avoid the inevitable gauntlet of questions, the prying eyes of the Mothers of the Church, their comments on Terry's absence, their observations on my altered appearance. I stared at my reflection, a stranger staring back, and whispered a desperate affirmation: "You got this." The empty church parking lot, a brief respite, offered a moment of false tranquility. "Thank you, Lord," I murmured, a fleeting sense of relief. I walked, a solitary figure, towards the choir stand, bracing myself for the arrival of the 'messy choir members.'

The choir room, a space of supposed harmony, filled with the discordant energy of unspoken tensions. The choir members and the choir director assembled in the choir room. The choir director, his eyes scanning the room, asked for a volunteer to lead prayer. A surge of unexpected resolve coursed through me. "I will pray," I stated, my voice firm, unwavering. A collective stillness fell over the room, a mixture of surprise and curiosity in their eyes. We joined hands, a fragile circle of forced unity. And then, I prayed.

Oh Heavenly Father, I thank you for your grace and mercy.

I thank you for this choir and the leader who directs this choir.

I pray that when we lift our voices to you, it will minister to someone's soul.

Lord, let the members of this choir know they have

a responsibility and that responsibility is to serve and honor you.

Father, we surrender to you in this ministry. Amen

The words, once a rote recitation, now carried a weight of raw emotion, a plea for understanding, a silent acknowledgment of the pain that lingered beneath the surface. It was a prayer not just for them, but for myself, a desperate attempt to find solace in the midst of chaos.

Their faces, a tableau of stunned disbelief, confirmed my suspicions. They expected a venomous sermon, a public airing of grievances. Instead, I offered a prayer, a plea for grace, a testament to the strength I clung to. "No weapon formed against me shall prosper," I whispered, a silent declaration of defiance. As the praise and worship began, a fragile sense of peace settled over me, a temporary reprieve from the storm raging within. Then, he walked in. Terry, radiating an unsettling charm, a picture of polished perfection. He moved through the sanctuary, shaking hands, flashing smiles, a performance of piety that twisted the knife in my already wounded heart. I forced my gaze away, focusing on the sanctuary, trying to find solace in the music. But then, the church announcer asked the visitors to stand, and there she was, standing beside him. His new girlfriend, brazenly displayed in the very place we had shared so many Sundays. The audacity of it, the sheer, unmitigated disrespect, sent a wave of heat through me. I felt the eyes of the congregation, their silent judgment, their morbid curiosity. My skin flushed, and sweat beaded on my forehead. A choir member, sensing my distress, passed me a handkerchief. "Get it together," I hissed under my breath, a desperate attempt to regain control. "Get it together."

It was time to take up the offering, and as if the technology team knew precisely what I needed to hear, Le'Andria Johnson's "Bigger Than Me" began to play, a welcome distraction from the inferno raging within. *He better be glad I'm in this choir stand,* I thought, a surge of vengeful anger coursing through me. As the choir prepared to sit with the congregation, I made my move, intending to position myself directly behind them, a silent declaration of my presence. But the head usher, her eyes sharp with unspoken warnings, intercepted me. "Sister, please sit on the other side of the church" she requested, her tone firm, unwavering. "When did we assign seats?" I asked, my voice laced with thinly veiled sarcasm. She offered no explanation, merely repeated her request. I complied, but my anger simmered, a volcano threatening to erupt. I followed her, and I could not wait until church was over. The head usher wanted to explain her reason for me not sitting behind Terry and his girlfriend. I knew she was attempting to shield me from witnessing their departure, a futile attempt to control the inevitable. I waited, my eyes fixed on the exit, and then, they were gone. His car, a symbol of their freedom, vanished into the traffic. A wave of rage, disappointment, hurt, and shame washed over me. I dialed his number, a desperate attempt to reclaim some semblance of control, but he didn't answer. I needed to escape, to find some semblance of normalcy, so I headed to the grocery store. And there they were, stopped at a red light, three cars ahead. The sight of them, so casually intertwined, ignited a firestorm of fury within me. As the light turned green, he sped away, a cowardly retreat. "'Oh, so you're going to speed up?" I seethed, my foot pressing harder on the gas. "But you were confident enough to bring her to church?" My phone rang, my friend's voice a desperate plea for calm, but I couldn't hear her. I was consumed by a blinding rage. "I'm going to confront him," I yelled into the phone, my voice raw with fury.

I was on his tail, a predator in pursuit, fueled by a rage that threatened to consume me. "I'm going to get him," I snarled into the phone, my voice a low, guttural growl. My friend's voice, sharp and urgent, cut through my fury. "Stop!" she commanded, the single word a jolt of ice water against my burning skin. And something shifted. The raw, animalistic rage that had gripped me began to recede, replaced by a bone-deep weariness. I pulled over, the car shuddering to a halt, as Terry's taillights vanished into the distance, a symbol of his continued escape. "It's not over," I whispered, a hollow promise to myself. My friend, her voice laced with concern, asked for my location, a silent acknowledgment of my unraveling. She arrived quickly, a familiar presence in the chaos of my despair. I stood on the side of the road, a broken figure, and unleashed a cry that was different from any I had uttered before. It wasn't just grief or anger; it was the sound of someone pushed beyond their breaking point, the raw, primal scream of a soul stripped bare. Finally, I allowed her to guide me home, her presence a fragile anchor in the storm. She stayed, her silent vigil a testament to her unwavering support, a silent guard against my own self-destruction. As soon as she left, I couldn't bear the weight of my clothes, the physical manifestation of the filth and cheapness I felt inside. I needed to cleanse myself, to wash away the stain of his betrayal. I needed a hot shower.

4

The Shower (The Turning Point)

Embarrassment, raw and searing, mixed with the stinging spray of the shower. The water, a relentless torrent, felt like heavy raindrops, each drop a fresh assault on my already bruised spirit. The harder the water fell, the deeper my anger burned. I sobbed, a child's desperate wail, echoing in the sterile confines of the bathroom. "How did I get here?" I cried, the question a hollow echo in the steam-filled air. Successful, intelligent, outgoing, giving—these were the words that once defined me. Now, I was a broken reflection, allowing a man to dictate my very essence. I was MADD—Mortified, Abandoned, Damaged, Dangerous—a volatile cocktail of emotions threatening to consume me. Normally, the shower was my sanctuary, a place of prayer and meditation, a space where I could reconnect with my faith. But now, silence. An oppressive, suffocating silence. I couldn't pray. The words, usually a lifeline, refused to form. "What's happening to me?" I whispered, fear coiling in my gut.

The only phrase that echoed in my mind, a hollow, desperate plea, was "Our Father, Our Father, Our Father." I tried to conjure a praise song, a melody to lift my spirits, but my mind was a blank canvas, devoid of inspiration. The shower's onslaught intensified, the water now a physical manifestation of my inner turmoil. And then, a whisper, a faint melody that pierced the silence: Anita Baker and the Winans. "Ain't no need in worrying, what the night is gonna bring, it'll be all over in the morning." I tried to scream, to release the pent-up anguish, but my voice was lost, swallowed by the steam and the relentless spray. I was emotionally drained, a hollow shell, yet the tears continued to flow, an unstoppable torrent. The song, a fragile lifeline, continued to play in my mind, the lyrics a soothing balm to my wounded soul. "Troubles come, but they do pass, heartaches, hurts, oh but, they don't last always. Sometimes we feel pain, but there are things that we can change, just pray." The words, a gentle reminder of faith's enduring power, began to calm the storm within. The tension in my shoulders eased, and the tightness in my chest loosened. Finally, I found my voice, a whisper at first, then a steady, unwavering prayer. "God," I pleaded, "give me the strength to get off this bathroom floor."

My name, a gentle echo, broke through the fog of my despair. I called back, my voice weak, letting her know I was emerging from the shower, a broken vessel pieced back together with fragile threads. My body, still heavy with the weight of my emotions, moved with a limped reluctance. I thanked God for her, a sanctuary of unwavering acceptance, a friend with whom I could lay bare my soul, both literally and figuratively. She didn't judge, didn't flinch, didn't offer empty platitudes. She simply listened, a silent guardian against the darkness that threatened to consume me. And then, she made me laugh. A soft chuckle at first, then a full-bodied release of tension, a sound I hadn't heard in days. "Were you going to hit the back of Terry's car?" she asked, her voice laced with a playful incredulity. I stared at her, a flicker of surprise in my eyes. "'No," I admitted, a slow realization dawning. "I didn't know what I was going to do." I only knew that I was MADD. Mortified, Abandoned, Damaged, Dangerous. The acronym, once a weapon of self-destruction, now hung in the air, a shared joke, a fragile bridge between our worlds. And then, we laughed again, a sound of healing, a testament to the power of connection. I was mortified, yes, just utterly embarrassed.

More than anything, I was mortified by the sheer audacity of it. The man I loved, the man I respected, had paraded his new girlfriend through the very sanctuary he knew was my refuge, my safe haven. The place where we had shared every Sunday, every service, every moment of connection. "Do you have a heart at all, Terry?" I whispered, the question a hollow echo in the quiet room. The image of his smile, a picture of smug contentment, replayed in my mind, a cruel mockery of the smiles we had shared as a couple. "Oh, how utterly ashamed I am," I groaned, the words a raw expression of my humiliation. Why the church, Terry? Why the place where I worshipped, where I poured out my heart in ministry, where we were supposed to begin our forever? I felt a physical ache, a tearing sensation in my chest, as if my very being was being ripped apart. Abandoned. Yes, abandoned. Left without protection, without care, without even a shred of decency. Did I mean anything to him? Was I just a fleeting amusement, a temporary distraction? Was I truly the 'nag' he had painted me to be? Why would he discard me so carelessly, so callously? "Help me, God," I cried, my voice raw with desperation. "What is wrong with me?" He had traded me for a stranger, a woman who didn't know his soul, who couldn't decipher his dry humor, who wouldn't know how to cradle his vulnerability. "God, do you hear me?" I pleaded. "He has abandoned me. Who will protect him now? I was his shield, his champion, the one who believed in his dreams when no one else did." And then, the tears returned, a flood of salty anguish, each drop a testament to the damage he had inflicted.

My blood pressure surged, a physical manifestation of the stress, the betrayal, the sheer, unmitigated cruelty of his actions. "Who am I?" I whispered, my voice trembling. "What do I believe?" The thought of ever trusting again, of ever loving again, felt like an impossible feat. He had shattered my perception of reality, leaving me adrift in a sea of doubt and pain. "I love you, only you," I mimicked, his voice a cruel echo in my mind. 'I want to make you happy. Thanks for being in my life." Lies. All lies. He was a liar, a deceiver, a destroyer of hearts.

I was spiraling, a vortex of rage and despair pulling me under. My thoughts, once rational and controlled, now twisted into dark, violent shapes. I felt myself slipping, becoming a stranger to myself, a danger to myself, perhaps even to Terry. "It's all your fault, Terry," I snarled, the words a venomous hiss in the quiet room. A darkness was rising within me, a primal rage I had never known. I was consumed by a daze, a red haze of fury, and I saw fire, an inferno of pain and betrayal that no earthly force could extinguish. I felt my girlfriend's hands on my shoulders, shaking me, her voice a distant echo. "What's wrong?" I managed, my voice hollow, detached. She described me as a blank sheet of paper, an empty vessel. I had checked out, disconnected from reality, lost in the labyrinth of my own rage. I was MADD—Mortified, Abandoned, Damaged, Dangerous— and I was teetering on the edge of something terrifying.

My girlfriend finally snapped me back to reality with a jolt of dark humor. "Girl," she said, her eyes wide, "you were about to lose it in that choir stand. You turned three shades darker, and your hands were clenched into fists like you were ready to fight. And then, after the song, you practically shoved those choir members out of the way – the ones who were talking mess about you at practice." She paused, her voice dropping. "I knew you were way past your limit when you tried to sit right behind Terry and his new girlfriend. I had to call in reinforcements. "She gestured towards the head usher, who stood nearby, her expression a mix of concern and lingering fear. "Ironic, isn't it'" she said, a wry smile twisting her lips. "You were so far gone, you didn't even see me." I stared at her, my mind a blank slate, devoid of any recollection. "I don't remember anything after leaving the choir stand," I admitted, my voice a hollow echo.

She proceeded to recount the whispers of the Mothers of the Church, their hushed warnings, their fear-filled pronouncements. "They asked me to stop you'" she said, her voice heavy with the weight of their terror. "They thought you were going to do something...horrible...to Terry" She paused, letting the word hang in the air. "They told him and his girlfriend to leave through the side door. Run like hell." I was stunned, disoriented. Was I truly capable of such rage? Had I become so consumed by my pain that I had transformed into something unrecognizable? "All of this happened around me?" I whispered, my voice trembling. *Was I truly that MADD?* The questions swirled in my mind, a chaotic vortex of confusion and self-doubt. What had he done to me? What had I become? And most importantly, what would I do next?

5

A Blank Sheet of Paper

T he phrase echoed, a hollow, mocking clang inside my skull: "A blank sheet of paper." It wasn't just words; it was a physical blow, a chilling draft that seeped into my bones. I stared at the pristine white surface of the notebook on the floor, the blankness mirroring the gaping void inside me.

"A blank sheet of paper," I whispered, the words tasting like ash. I'd looked up the definition, a clinical, sterile explanation: *a sheet of paper devoid of markings.* And in that moment, it wasn't just paper. It was me. Utterly, devastatingly empty.

Am I nothing? The question clawed at my throat, a feral thing desperate to be heard. *Is that all I was to him? A blank space to be filled, a temporary placeholder until something... better... came along?*

My best friend's words, meant to be a brutal, necessary truth, now twisted into a weapon. "Place-holding." "Space-filling." The phrases swirled, a nauseating vortex. I remembered the way Terry had said, "I need space," his voice distant, detached. *Space-filling.* Like I was some kind of emotional caulking, plugging up the cracks until he found something more substantial.

The room seemed to shrink, the walls closing in. The air grew thick, suffocating. I crumpled to the floor, the cold tile a stark contrast to the burning in my chest. *Get off this floor,* I screamed internally, but my limbs were leaden, unresponsive.

Tears streamed down my face, hot and furious, blurring the edges of the world. My sobs were ragged, animalistic, the sound of something breaking. *Hopeless.* That's what I was. Utterly, irrevocably hopeless.

I wanted to call my girlfriend, to hear a voice, any voice, but the thought was a fresh wave of pain. She was tired of this, tired of my endless loop of despair. And she, of all people, had seen me as a blank sheet of paper. She'd understood the inherent emptiness before I did.

Who can I talk to? The question hung in the air, unanswered. They wouldn't understand. They'd see the cracks, the unraveling edges, and label me "crazy." *Maybe I am crazy,* I thought, a dark, insidious whisper.

The emotions, raw and untamed, surged through me, a tidal wave threatening to drown me. I was adrift, lost in a sea of nothingness. *Who?* The word echoed in the silence, a desperate, unanswered plea. *Who can I turn to?* The question, a raw, bleeding wound, remained suspended in the suffocating air, unanswered, a testament to my utter isolation.

The chaos in my mind raged, a hurricane of "what ifs" and "why me's." I felt like a puppet with cut strings, adrift and useless. But somewhere, deep beneath the layers of despair, a flicker of something else stirred. I remembered a voice, a promise.

I sank to my knees, the cold floor grounding me, and began to speak, the words broken, ragged. "God... you said... Matthew 7:7-8..." The verses, once a source of comfort, now felt like a desperate plea, a lifeline thrown into a raging sea.

"Ask… and it will be given… seek… and you will find… knock… and the door will be opened…" Each word was a struggle, a battle against the crushing weight of my despair. "I thought… I thought I had found him, God. I thought Terry… he was the answer. But the door… it opened wide, then slammed shut. I'm so tired. So tired of this."

My voice cracked, tears blurring my vision. "What kind of storm is this? One minute, sunshine… the next, a raging tempest? I don't understand." The questions were hurled into the silence, unanswered, raw with pain and confusion.

A wave of nausea washed over me, a stark reminder of my physical neglect. I hadn't eaten, hadn't moved, just existed in this vortex of grief. *I need to eat,* a small, rational voice whispered, a fragile counterpoint to the chaos.

I dragged myself up, the room swaying slightly. *I can't face people.* The thought was a visceral rejection, a need to retreat, to shield myself from the world's prying eyes. *Drive-thru,* I decided, the words a mantra. *Just a drive-thru. No talking. No explanations.* Just the anonymity of a car window and a paper bag, a small, temporary barrier against the overwhelming weight of my emptiness. I was a broken thing, clinging to the smallest semblance of control, a blank sheet of paper, crumpled and torn, seeking a moment's respite from the storm.

The drive-thru line stretched endlessly, a slow, agonizing crawl. But time was all I had, a vast, empty expanse mirroring the hollowness within me. No one waited at home, no warm lights, no comforting sounds. Just an empty apartment, a silent testament to my solitude.

Finally, I reached the window, and my heart sank. *Of all people.* My noisy neighbor, the one with the perpetual smirk and the insatiable need to know everyone's business, was working the drive-thru. The universe, it seemed, was determined to mock my misery.

She leaned forward, her eyes bright with a cruel curiosity. "Your boyfriend was just here," she stated, the words flat, devoid of any pretense of sympathy.

My breath hitched. *He was here? With her?*

"With another woman," she added, her eyes gleaming with morbid curiosity. "And you know, I haven't seen him at your place lately."

The audacity of her words, the sheer invasive cruelty, sent a wave of white-hot rage through me. *Stick to the script,* I seethed internally. *It's my pleasure to serve you, not your pleasure to dissect my life.*

A dark, impulsive thought flickered: *Ask her what she looked like. How long ago did they leave? I could catch them, make them both pay.* But the image of a confrontation, of exposing my raw pain, was too much. I couldn't give her the satisfaction.

My heart pounded against my ribs, a frantic drumbeat against my fragile composure. I could feel the rise and fall of my chest, the rapid, shallow breaths betraying my inner turmoil. *Does everyone know?* The thought was a chilling wave of paranoia. *Is this some kind of public spectacle?*

He's with her all the time. The realization was a sharp, agonizing twist of the knife. My world, already shattered, splintered further. I was trapped, exposed, a raw nerve in the middle of a crowded street, and my neighbor, the ultimate voyeur, was reveling in my pain. I wanted to scream, to shatter the glass separating us, but I was frozen, trapped in a silent scream of utter devastation.

Hmmmm.... A dark, reckless impulse surged through me. *I'll just drive by his place. See if they're there. Just a peek.* I grabbed my food, the greasy paper bag a flimsy shield against the storm raging inside me, and peeled out of the drive-thru, the tires squealing in protest.

Adrenaline coursed through my veins, a dangerous cocktail of rage and desperation. I pressed the gas pedal, the world blurring around me. My phone rang, a jarring intrusion, and I glanced down, realizing I was speeding, a dangerous, reckless speed. I forced myself to slow down, answering the call with a trembling hand.

"Turn that car around," my girlfriend's voice commanded, sharp and unwavering.

"What? Where are you?" I stammered, confused. "I'm on my way home."

I glanced in the rearview mirror, and my blood ran cold. Her car was there, close behind, a silent, menacing presence. *What in the world?* I was beyond frustrated, beyond exhausted. This felt like a violation.

The traffic light turned red, trapping me. She pulled up beside me, her expression grim. She motioned for me to roll down my window. "Follow me," she said, her voice leaving no room for argument.

Dang, follow you? A wave of resentment washed over me. *Does she think I'm going to church? Because that's definitely not happening.*

I reluctantly drove my car, following her to her house. She feigned a casualness that rang false, claiming she'd just seen me and wanted to "hang out." But I knew the truth. She'd seen the fire in my eyes, the reckless determination, and she was intervening, pulling me back from the precipice.

I played along, a fragile truce in a war zone, but the unspoken threat hung heavy in the air. We both knew the truth. She had stopped me from a confrontation, and I was boiling.

The conversation flowed, a fragile bridge across the chasm of my despair. For a while, I even managed to laugh, a rusty, unfamiliar sound. Then, the question, sharp and insistent, pierced the fragile peace: "What did you mean, 'blank sheet of paper' at church?"

Confusion flickered across her face. "What are you talking about?"

"Was I just a placeholder for Terry?" I asked, my voice tight. "Is that why you said I looked like a blank sheet of paper?"

She was dumbfounded, her eyes wide with bewildered concern. "Do you... do you need to see a counselor?"

"Hell no," I snapped, the defensive wall rising instantly. "Just answer the question. I'm a licensed psychologist, for crying out loud. I'd know if I needed counseling."

Seeing my rising agitation, she softened. "Look, when I said that... you read way too much into it." "Of course, you'd say that," I muttered, but the relief was a subtle, insidious thing. We talked more, the conversation circling back to the core of my pain.

"Am I crazy?" I asked, the question hanging in the air, raw and vulnerable. "No," she said firmly. "You're a woman who loves hard and didn't get that love returned."

"Yes," I breathed, the validation a balm to my wounded soul. "Just... bear with me. I'll get better. It's just... one day, engagement, the next, 'I need space.' And to know... he was already in another relationship..."

I knew she saw the cracks, the barely concealed unraveling. And deep down, I knew it too. *I think I need help, but I can't admit it.* I was losing my grip.

"Can you believe I took that 'blank sheet of paper' thing so seriously?" I said, a bitter laugh escaping me. "I'm losing it."

I need to do something nice for her, I thought. *Who else would put up with this?*

The conversation had calmed the storm, pushed back the darkness. *She saved me again,* I thought, a wave of gratitude washing over me. But as I prepared to leave, she smiled, a knowing, almost pleading smile. "Don't go by Terry's house."

The words were a jolt, a sharp reminder of the raw, exposed nerve. *Are you serious?* I'd been doing so well, but now, the temptation, the need to know, surged back.

Am I really a blank sheet of paper? The question echoed in my mind.

I gave her a tight, fake smile. "I'm not going. I have my own house. I don't care what he's doing."

I repeated the words in my head, a mantra, but the doubt gnawed at me, a persistent, insidious fear. *I don't believe myself.*

The speed limit signs blurred, meaningless markers in my escalating rage. My foot pressed the gas pedal, the car hurtling forward, a block, then half a block, then... Terry's street. A line of cars snaked along the curb, their presence a physical blow.

Fear, cold and sharp, pierced my anger. I didn't dare roll down the window, afraid of being recognized, of exposing my vulnerability. *He's having a party?* The thought was a sickening wave of disbelief. *He never did this when we were together.*

I killed my headlights, creeping forward, a ghost in the night. I strained to see into the darkness, to identify the vehicles. *Please, no one I know.* But fate, it seemed, had other plans. A co-worker's car, then a church member's. My stomach churned. The music pulsed, a heavy, throbbing beat, and smoke curled from the back of the house.

I should go back there, a dark, reckless voice whispered. *Surprise!* But my girlfriend's warning echoed in my ears, a stark reminder of my fragile control.

I'll stop the party, I decided, a surge of vindictive energy coursing through me. I drove around the corner, parked, and dialed 911. My voice trembled as I tried to explain, but the music drowned out my words. "Loud music... can't sleep..." I managed to convey, the lie a bitter taste in my mouth.

The operator dispatched officers, and moments later, the flashing lights of three police cars filled the street. My stomach flipped, a wave of nausea washing over me. *What have I done?*

The music abruptly stopped, and a tense silence fell. I waited, holding my breath, but no one left. Then, the music started again, louder, more defiant. *You've got to be kidding me.*

I drove back around the corner. The police cars were still there, and the party seemed to have grown. *They joined the party?* The realization was a crushing blow. I drove away, a raw, animalistic rage building inside me.

Back at my apartment, I paced, a caged animal. *He's having a party. With people I know.* The betrayal was a physical ache, a gaping wound in my soul. *The police did nothing.*

I'm a blank sheet of paper, I thought, the phrase echoing in my mind, a hollow, mocking sound. *I'm nothing. I meant nothing to him.*

Tears streamed down my face, hot and furious. *He's moved on. And I'm here, sobbing over a man who never cared.* The truth, stark and brutal, crashed over me. *I was in a relationship by myself.* The realization was a devastating, final blow, leaving me shattered and alone.

The sobs wouldn't stop, a raw, animalistic sound that tore through the silence of my apartment. I just wanted to sleep, to escape into oblivion, but the nightmare clung to me, a suffocating shroud. The alarm blared, a cruel reminder of the new week, the new reality.

I wanted to call my girlfriend, to scream, to unleash the fury that simmered within me, but I knew she'd see the madness, the desperate act of calling the police, and lock me away. So, I braced myself, a soldier heading into battle, for the Monday morning gossip session at work.

As I walked into the office, my co-worker, the one whose car I'd seen at Terry's, was holding court, entertaining everyone with tales of the party. I forced myself to the front desk, to listen, to glean every painful detail.

And then," he said, his voice laced with excitement, "three police cars showed up! Terry was so confused. He'd told the neighbors about the party, so he knew they hadn't called."

My breath hitched.

The room spun. I almost collapsed. Propose? My world shattered, the pieces falling around me like broken glass. I forced myself to stay upright, to maintain a facade of composure.

"It was beautiful," he said, his voice dripping with saccharine sweetness. "They didn't leave until

it was over."

I stumbled to my office, the world a blur of pain and betrayal. I curled into my chair, a broken doll, trapped in a silent scream. Nowhere to hide. Nowhere to run.

I called my girlfriend, my voice trembling. "He proposed… to someone else."

Her lack of surprise was a fresh wave of agony. She knew.

"Why didn't you tell me?" I whispered, the words thick with betrayal.

Silence stretched between us, a chasm of unspoken truths. My best friend, the one who knew me better than anyone, had kept this from me. Done. I hung up, ignoring the barrage of calls and texts that followed.

A blank sheet of paper. The phrase echoed in my mind, a cruel, mocking epitaph. Terry, the charming, loving man, had played me for a fool. He needed space... from me.

A chilling realization washed over me. I was adrift, cut off from the world, utterly alone. How am I going to get through this? Hopeless and dismayed, I stared into the abyss, the question hanging in the air, unanswered, a dark, ominous promise of the chaos to come.

6

The Silent Fall

"Dear God," I whispered, my voice hoarse, a raw, ragged sound, "please order my steps. Because I am so messed up right now." The bathroom tiles were cold against my skin, a stark contrast to the burning in my chest. "I put Terry before you. I lost my footing with you. I'm broken, God. So, confused."

You said you'd never leave me, I thought, the words a desperate plea. So, what happened? He was supposed to be my man. "Hold my hand, God," I sobbed, tears blurring my vision. "I feel so alone. I need you to rock me in your bosom."

The world seemed to tilt, the edges of reality blurring. I stared at the bathroom floor, the grout lines a map of my despair. This girl is broken. "Jesus," I whispered, the name a lifeline. "I'm depending on you to get me through this storm. 'With God all things are possible.' Matthew 19:26." But the words felt hollow, a distant echo in the vast emptiness of my soul.

I stumbled toward the mirror, my reflection a stranger. I recoiled, a gasp escaping my lips. Who is this? The face staring back was gaunt, the skin sallow, the eyes dark and sunken. My hair, once vibrant, now hung limp and lifeless. I don't know who I am anymore.

I slid to the floor, the cold tile a comforting weight. How did I let myself get here? Twenty pounds heavier, a testament to the emotional void I tried to fill with food, or the lack of it, I couldn't tell. Sleep was a distant memory, replaced by endless nights of torment.

My phone lay silent, the screen dark. The blocked contact of my best friend, the one I used to share everything with, was a constant, painful reminder of my isolation. Too ashamed to reveal the depth of my despair, I continued the charade, the mask of normalcy a heavy, suffocating weight. I couldn't even reach out to the one person who might understand.

But beneath the surface, a flicker of something else stirred. I thought of the butterfly, its metamorphosis a slow, painful transformation. Larvae to caterpillar to chrysalis to winged adult. A complete transformation. Maybe… maybe there's hope for me too.

Like the caterpillar, I had retreated into my chrysalis, a dark, silent space of isolation. But the thought of emerging, of spreading my wings and flying, was a fragile, desperate hope. *Metamorphosis.* The word echoed in my mind, a promise of change, of a future beyond this pain. But the journey was long, and the darkness was deep. Could I truly transform? Could I break free from this shell of despair, even with no one to help me? The question hung in the air, unanswered, a fragile seed of hope in the desolate landscape of my broken heart.

Pupa. The word echoed in my mind, a clinical term for a state of transformation, yet it felt disturbingly accurate. I was encased in a self-made chrysalis, my skin darkening, mirroring the internal decay. The vibrant woman I once was, the one who frequented the salon weekly, was fading, replaced by a shadow of herself.

The constant hum of gossip, the whispers about Terry and his fiancé, was a relentless assault, a daily reminder of my shattered reality. To shield myself, I retreated further, investing in wigs, each one a mask, a temporary escape from the pain.

Each wig, a "WIG" (Woman Is Going-Thru), was a tangible representation of my fractured emotional state. I named them, imbued them with the essence of my suffering.

Diverse: The 30-inch deep wave lace front. It was my anchor, my illusion of strength. It represented the "very strong bond founded on deep feelings of dependency and need" that had ensnared me. I'd been "in too deep," my attachment to Terry a toxic tendril, binding me on an emotional and physiological level I couldn't comprehend. It was the wig I wore when I needed to feel like I could still be loved.

Mysterious: The short bob with the bangs. It was the embodiment of my confusion, my desperate plea for understanding. It represented the "hurt when someone who loved you and committed to you decided to throw in the towel." *Why wasn't I enough?* The question echoed in the sharp, angular cut of the wig, a constant, silent accusation.

Camouflaged: The 360 wig. It was a chaotic swirl of emotions, a constant, dizzying shift. One moment, I felt a fragile sense of progress, the next, I was spiraling back into despair. It was the "constant change during the day," the "camouflaged" reality of my life, a facade masking the turmoil beneath. One moment I felt like I was healing, the next I was right back where I started.

Each wig was a layer of armor, a desperate attempt to piece together the shattered fragments of my identity. But beneath the carefully styled strands, the pain remained, a raw, festering wound. I was a pupa, trapped in a self-made prison, waiting, hoping for a transformation that felt impossibly distant.

Each morning was a battle, each step a Herculean effort.

What is wrong with me? The question echoed in the hollow spaces of my mind. Makeup, once a tool of confidence, now failed to conceal the dark circles, the telltale signs of sleepless nights and endless tears. My clothes hung loosely, shapeless and drab, like relics from a past life.

I traveled, seeking solace in new landscapes, but the pain was a constant companion, a shadow that stretched across every horizon. Every couple I saw, every shared smile, was a cruel reminder of what I had lost.

Returning home was a descent into darkness. The bathroom floor, my sanctuary of despair, became my nightly ritual. I wept until my contacts blurred, until my eyes were swollen and raw. Will this pain ever end?

My strength, once rooted in faith, had withered. I couldn't bear the thought of church, of facing Terry and his fiancé, of enduring the well-meaning but agonizing questions of the church mothers. And the choir, my refuge, was now a source of unbearable pain.

I'm losing myself, I thought, a wave of panic washing over me. I need God. The realization was a stark, painful truth. I couldn't let Terry steal my faith, my sanctuary. I decided, with a fragile resolve, to return to church, to reclaim my life.

Another week, another battle against the shifting sands of "Camouflaged." At work, the whispers about Terry continued, but I held my head high, clinging to the promise of Isaiah 54:17. "No weapon formed against me shall prosper." I was stronger, wiser, though still wounded. A small victory: a week without collapsing on the bathroom floor.

The weekend arrived, a brief respite. I drove along Interstate 20, a sense of fragile freedom washing over me. A good day, I thought, a rare, precious moment. But as I neared my neighborhood, the familiar silhouette of Terry's car shattered the illusion.

Why is he here? Panic flared, a primal fear of being pulled back into the abyss. No. Not tonight. I bypassed my house, heading for the store, desperate to avoid a confrontation.

But fate, it seemed, had other plans. Terry's car appeared at the next traffic light. He looked… good. Too good. The familiar pull, the longing, threatened to overwhelm me. Not tonight, I repeated, a desperate mantra.

Back at my house, preparing for church, the image of Terry at the light haunted me. The self-talk, the fragile defenses, were crumbling. I refuse to fall apart. But the battle was far from over, and the threat of relapse loomed, a dark, ominous cloud.

Sunday. The ultimate test. I was determined to face the lion's den, but from the relative safety of the balcony. It took an eternity to reach the church, each mile a battle against my own fear. The parking lot was a sea of cars, and I scanned it, a desperate search for Terry's.

He's here. The confirmation was a jolt, a physical blow.

As I approached the door, the greeters' eyes widened, their expressions a mix of shock and morbid curiosity. I saw them whispering to security. They want to use their power today? I thought, a surge of defiant anger. Not today.

I retreated to the balcony, my vantage point, and there they were: Terry and his fiancé, dressed in matching outfits. Like twins. A wave of bitterness washed over me. He hated when I suggested matching colors.

I wore "Diverse," my armor, but anxiety gnawed at me, a relentless predator. Tears streamed down my face, but I forced myself to focus on the One audience that mattered. Jesus.

The choir director spotted me, and the irony was almost unbearable. They began to sing "You Will Win." "I know you are hurt, I know you are torn, I know you are broken, but you will win". The lyrics were a raw, painful truth, a lifeline in the swirling darkness.

My best friend joined me, her presence a balm to my wounded soul. I had been cruel, distant, and I knew I owed her an apology. Life is tough, but I must praise God for the small victories.

The pastor's sermon was a direct hit, each word a carefully aimed arrow. Is he spying on me? Paranoia flared, a hot, prickly sensation. Who has he been talking to? I wanted to scream, to accuse him of using the pulpit as a weapon, but my friend's gentle touch calmed me. I'm okay. I'm okay.

I clung to that mantra, refusing to succumb to the darkness. I won't go back to the bathroom floor. He won't determine my destiny.

When the pastor called for altar call, my friend asked me to go. For prayer. I hesitated, then followed her, the eyes of the congregation burning into me. Weakness. I felt it creeping in, threatening to consume me.

But as the pastor prayed, his words were a torrent of strength, a balm to my wounded spirit. Tears flowed freely, a release, a cleansing. The Holy Spirit moved, a tangible presence, a lifeline in the midst of my despair. The Holy Spirit moved, a tangible presence, a lifeline in the midst of my despair. Then, the world tilted, and I felt myself being lifted from the floor.

When I regained my footing, disoriented, I prepared to return to my seat. But Terry stood in the center aisle, blocking my path.

Nowhere to go but towards him. My mind raced, a chaotic jumble of emotions. I wasn't even sure if my wig was still secure.

As I approached, he extended his arms, a gesture of... what? Satan, get behind me. Was he toying with me? Why would I want to hug him? I braced myself, a silent plea for divine intervention.

But my legs betrayed me. I stumbled forward, falling directly into his embrace. The sanctuary fell silent, the weight of their gaze pressing down on me.

He pulled away, his voice low and strained. "My fiancé is behind you."

What? The word echoed in the sudden silence, a raw, incredulous sound. I felt a surge of pure, unadulterated rage.

I fled, running from the church, my girlfriend close behind. I slammed the car door, the engine roaring to life, a desperate escape. I made a fool of myself. The thought was a searing brand on my soul.

Back at my apartment, I collapsed, the world spinning. I was violently ill, sweat slicking my skin, my hands trembling. Losing my grip. I was an emotional wreck, a shattered vessel.

I lay on the bathroom floor, unable to move, and called my girlfriend. "Help me," I whispered, my voice weak. She helped me up, and I stumbled into the shower, desperate to wash away the phantom scent of Terry. Ninety minutes I stood there, scrubbing, but the memory, the humiliation, clung to me like a second skin.

My girlfriend kept coming into the bathroom, checking on me, her presence a silent, unwavering support. Emerging from the shower, I was weak, drained, but the physical cleansing offered a sliver of relief. My girlfriend could only hold me, her embrace a silent expression of her deep empathy. She felt my pain as if it were her own. I tried to explain, to convince us both, that I was making progress. I told her about seeing Terry in my neighborhood, how I'd resisted the urge to follow him. I told her I was reclaiming my life, refusing to be defined by this desperation. She cried with me, her tears a testament to her unwavering support. But the events of church, the public humiliation, had shattered my fragile composure. I knew, with a certainty that chilled me to the bone, that I couldn't face work tomorrow. No way could I endure the scrutiny of those 'monsters,' the co-workers who would dissect my pain. I was certain the entire city knew what had happened at church today, and I was exposed, vulnerable, and utterly broken.

Finally, I mustered the strength to look at my phone. Twenty-seven missed calls.

Twenty-seven? My heart pounded. I scrolled through the list, a mix of dread and morbid curiosity. They weren't all from one person, a chaotic symphony of concern and, undoubtedly, gossip. I grasped for a lifeline, a sliver of sanity, and remembered the words of Psalms 27:1-3.

"The Lord is my light and my salvation; whom shall I fear? The Lord is the strength of my life; of whom shall I be afraid? When the wicked, even mine enemies and my foes, came upon me to eat up my flesh, they stumbled and fell. Though an host should encamp against me, my heart shall not fear: though war should rise against me, in this will I be confident."

I repeated the verses, each word a mantra, a shield against the encroaching darkness. Whom shall I fear? Stumbled and fell. In this will I be confident. The words resonated, a fragile promise of strength.

I will not be afraid. I declared, the words a silent vow. Not when I see them. Not ever again. I would not allow them to steal my peace, to dictate my well-being. I may stumble, I may fall, but I will rise. The battle is the Lord's, not mine.

Confidence. That was the key. Confidence in the face of chaos, in the midst of heartbreak. Confidence in my ability to navigate the wreckage of my life.

I shared my newfound resolve with my girlfriend, the words a fragile declaration of independence. She met my gaze, her expression unwavering. "So," she asked, her voice firm, "are you going to work tomorrow?"

"No," I replied, the word ringing with a newfound conviction. "No, I'm not."

I needed peace. A sanctuary, a space to process the events of the day, to rebuild the shattered fragments of my composure. I couldn't face the scrutiny, the prying eyes, until I had found some semblance of inner calm.

I'm not the only one, I thought, a bitter laugh escaping me. Not the only woman who's tried to diagnose herself from the DSM after a brutal breakup. The thought, though dark, offered a strange sense of solidarity. A shared experience in the wilderness of heartbreak. I needed time to heal, to find my footing, to reclaim my sanity. And I would not apologize for it.

Monday was a day of sanctuary, a day to piece together the fragments of myself. A day dedicated to preparing for "Therapeutic Tuesday." I knew the drill: Monday would be a feeding frenzy of gossip, and Tuesday would be a public observation, a collective assessment of my mental stability.

They want to see if I've cracked, I thought, a surge of defiant anger. They'll be disappointed.

It was time for a change, a visual declaration of my rebirth.

The wigs, my emotional masks, had served their purpose, but they were now tainted, reminders of my vulnerability. I needed something new, something vibrant. Color. I needed color.

"What does it mean when a woman goes blonde?" I typed into Google, a desperate search for meaning in the mundane. The results were a revelation: "Researchers have discovered that when you change your hair color, your personality changes as well. If you become a blonde, you're more likely to be more fun, more exuberant, and more concerned with your appearance."

Fun. Exuberant. Words that had been foreign to me for too long. This is what I need. A jolt of energy, a reclaiming of my lost sparkle. I wouldn't go platinum, but a touch of blonde, a hint of sunshine, was exactly what I needed.

I found it: an Ombre 24-inch body wave wig, a cascade of golden hues. Blon. I named her, a symbol of my newfound optimism. This is the new me. I felt a lightness, a sense of anticipation I hadn't experienced in weeks.

I called my girlfriend, her reaction a burst of laughter and relief. "Thank God," she exclaimed. "No more gloom and doom! You're finally getting some color back in your life!" "Miles to go," I admitted, "but this is a start."

"Are you ready for work tomorrow?" she asked, her voice laced with cautious optimism.

"Yes," I replied, a genuine smile spreading across my face.

She warned me about the inevitable barrage of questions, the concerned inquiries from church members. "They're just being nosy," I said, a flicker of irritation in my voice. "Especially the choir director and those ladies."

"They're worried," she insisted.

"Tell them to pray for themselves," I retorted, a surge of defiance in my voice. I'm not their spectacle. I'm not their project. I was reclaiming my narrative, rewriting my story, and I wouldn't let their pity or their gossip derail me. Blon was my armor, my shield, and I was ready for battle.

I arrived at work early, determined to control the narrative. I wouldn't give them the satisfaction of watching me navigate their judgmental stares. But they, the vultures, had anticipated my move, and beat me to it. Holy Ghost, help me walk through these doors.

I entered, head held high, and greeted them with a bright, almost manic, "Happy Therapeutic Tuesday!" Their faces registered confusion, a collective question mark.

"What do you want to know?" I asked, my voice sharp, cutting through the manufactured pleasantries. "What do you have to say?"

The silence was deafening. If I'd known being aggressive would shut them up, I'd have done this sooner. I retreated to my office, the battle won, but the war far from over. I filled the room with worship music, a shield against the lingering tension.

A knock. "Come in... at your own risk," I said, my voice laced with a dark humor.

The administrative assistant Lori entered, her face a mask of unspoken pain, a mirror of my own recent torment. I asked her what was wrong, but she couldn't speak. Tears streamed down her face, and then, with a choked sob, she crumpled to the floor.

Oh my God. The realization hit me like a physical blow. She was on the bathroom floor. A wave of empathy, raw and visceral, washed over me. I rushed to her side, pulling her into an embrace. Lori sobs intensified, a raw, primal sound that echoed through the office. Thank God for my music, masking the sound of her despair.

We sat there, in silence, two broken souls, a shared understanding that transcended words. The unspoken question hung heavy in the air: What had broken her? And how many more were suffering in silence?

7

You Are Not the Only One

I wasn't the only woman on the bathroom floor. The realization, once a distant echo, now resonated with a chilling clarity. I began to observe, to truly see, the women around me. In the grocery store, at church, in the mall, even at work, I could spot them. The telltale signs: the haunted eyes, the forced smiles, the invisible weight they carried. It was as if I'd developed a sixth sense, a radar for pain.

Women are emotional creatures, bound by invisible threads of connection. When we love, we love fiercely, deeply, irrevocably. And when those ties are severed, the pain is a raw, agonizing wound. I'd thought I was alone in my suffering, that no one could comprehend the depths of my despair. But I was wrong. The bathroom floor was a shared space, a desolate landscape we all traversed. I wouldn't wish that journey on my worst enemy. The pain, the self-doubt, the crippling darkness—it was an experience beyond words.

Day by day, I clawed my way forward, but the journey was a treacherous climb. My co-workers, the vultures, continued their whispers, their judgmental stares. But I'd learned to build walls, to create a space of emotional distance. And then there was Lori. She was a mirror, a reflection of my past self. Her forced cheerfulness, her darkening eyes, her sudden infatuation with wigs—it was a familiar pattern. She was in the beginning stages of transformation, trapped in the chrysalis of pain. I prayed for her, silently, respectfully, resisting the urge to offer unsolicited advice. I remembered how much I hated it when people did that to me.

My sanctuary was my music, the praise and worship that filled my office, creating a bubble of peace. I was focused, determined to maintain my composure. Then, my phone rang. I ignored it, but the insistent buzz of text messages followed. Finally, I succumbed, checking the screen. Terry. A missed call, two text messages.

Are you tripping? The audacity of it sent a jolt of adrenaline through me.

Psalms 27. I grasped for the familiar words, a lifeline in the swirling chaos. "The Lord is my light and my salvation; whom shall I fear?"

I read the texts. "I miss you. Can we talk?" He misses me? The words were a dangerous temptation, a siren's call. "I need to see you. I need to talk." The urgency in his words sent a thrill of excitement through me, a forbidden spark of hope. Closure. That's what I needed, right?

I called my girlfriend, her voice a voice of reason. "Don't respond," she warned.

But I couldn't resist. Just to see what happens. I texted back, and the floodgates opened. He wanted to come over, tonight. Yes.

72

The word echoed in my mind, a dangerous, reckless impulse. I need closure, I repeated, a desperate justification for my weakness. But deep down, I knew the truth. I was playing with fire, and I was about to get burned.

The drive home was a blur of anticipation, a dangerous cocktail of hope and denial. Terry arrived, and for hours, we talked, replaying the highlights of our past, the moments that still held a dangerous allure. He asked to stay the night, and a part of me, the vulnerable, desperate part, screamed yes. But the rational voice, the one still bruised and wary, whispered no.

He was incredulous. "Can we at least have lunch tomorrow?"

Yes. The word was a silent scream, a surrender to the dangerous pull. He's trying, I told myself, clinging to a fragile thread of hope. He apologized. I wouldn't tell my best friend. She'd see the folly of it, the reckless abandon, and try to stop me. But something, a dark, reckless impulse, compelled me to see where this led.

Lunch was a dream, a replay of our happiest moments. I feel like myself again, I thought, the feeling a dangerous, intoxicating high. My best friend called, her voice bright. "You sound happy," she said. "What's got you smiling?"

"The Lord," I replied, a half-truth, a shield against her inevitable disapproval. "I'll see you at church. Balcony seating."

Sunday. The ultimate test of my fragile resolve. The church mothers, ever eager to dispense unsolicited wisdom, met me in the parking lot. "You're brave to come back," one said, her voice laced with thinly veiled judgment. "But, baby, you made a fool of yourself." Respect your elders. The words were a bitter taste in my mouth. She knows exactly what she's doing.

Terry and his fiancé were there, a constant, painful reminder of my folly. He'll tell her, I thought, a desperate hope clinging to my heart. He'll tell her it was a mistake.

The secretary's announcements began, a droning litany of church events, but her voice held a strange, pointed emphasis. I felt her eyes, and the eyes of the congregation, drawn to the balcony, where I sat, exposed and vulnerable. Then came the final announcement, the one that shattered my fragile composure. 'Terry's wedding,' she declared, her voice ringing through the silent sanctuary, each word a hammer blow to my heart. 'December 9th. Everyone is invited.'

A collective gasp rippled through the pews. December 9th. The date echoed in my mind, a cruel, mocking reminder of my shattered dreams. He's been in my face, whispering sweet nothings, and he's getting married? The betrayal was a physical ache, a searing brand on my soul. The air thickened, heavy with unspoken judgment. I felt the weight of their stares, the pity, the morbid curiosity. A surge of rage, hot and violent, threatened to consume me. I wanted to scream, to shatter the stained-glass windows, to expose the hypocrisy that permeated the room.

Security stood near the aisle, their presence a silent warning. Not another scene, I thought, a desperate plea for control. Don't give them the satisfaction. But the humiliation was a raw, gaping wound, and the urge to lash out, to unleash the storm within me, was almost unbearable.

My best friend texted from the choir stand, her concern a silent accusation. "Are you okay?"

"No," I texted back, the word a raw, honest admission. "I'm MADD. He's doing this again. Trying to destroy me."

Church couldn't end fast enough. As I descended the stairs, Denise, a former church member, approached me. "Can we talk?" she asked, her eyes filled with an unsettling intensity.

Not now, I thought, but the pain in her eyes, a mirror of my own, compelled me to say yes. "Follow me," I said, my voice strained.

Driving home, I replayed the events, the betrayal a fresh wound. What is he trying to do? The urge to collapse, to retreat to the familiar comfort of the bathroom floor, was overwhelming. But Denise needed me, and I couldn't abandon her.

My best friend called, her voice laced with concern. "Are you okay?"

"Yes," I lied, the word a hollow echo. "I won't do anything stupid."

Back at my apartment, I finally succumbed, collapsing to my knees. But instead of the floor, I cried out to God, a raw, desperate plea. "You won't put more on me than I can handle!"

The doorbell rang. Denise stood on the porch, her eyes filled with an unspoken understanding. And in that moment, I knew I wasn't alone.

The pain in Denise's eyes was a mirror, reflecting my own shattered reality. "Do you need anything?" I asked, my voice soft, laced with a newfound empathy.

She broke down, her words a raw, desperate plea. "I need to get naked," she sobbed, "and you're the only person I can get naked with." The vulnerability in her voice was startling, a stark admission of the emotional stripping she'd endured. "I'm tired of pretending," she confessed, her voice thick with tears. "I'm on a roller coaster, and the dips and turns are making me sick."

I know that feeling, I thought, the words a silent echo of my own experience.

Denise began to unravel her story, a tale of a two-year relationship with her "soulmate." The perfect couple, I'd thought. The perfect gentleman. They traveled, attended events, and she'd even joined his church. They were the picture of devotion, destined for a Christmas engagement.

He was a pillar of the ministry, and she, with her passion and dedication, quickly found her place. The pastor, recognizing her talent, appointed her to oversee the Media Ministry, then, later, Public Relations. She was thrilled, brimming with ideas, eager to contribute to the kingdom.

She shared her enthusiasm with her soulmate, expecting his support. Instead, he met her excitement with a chilling indifference. "Don't you think you're doing too much?" he asked, his voice laced with a subtle, insidious jealousy. "You just joined the ministry, and you're trying to take over."

She brushed it off as a joke, but his words lingered, a subtle poison. He then told her "people in the church are talking about you. They asked me to talk to you, because you are moving too quickly."

The betrayal was a sharp, agonizing twist. Ouch. I understood that pain, the sting of being undermined by the one you trusted.

She continued to excel, refusing to let his negativity dim her light. But his resentment grew, festering into a raw, ugly thing. She smiled at him, a simple, warm expression that seemed to ask, *Doesn't this feel good? All this hard work paying off?* "Does it?" he hissed, his voice laced with contempt. "I'm tired of you trying to be a show-off at church. You're making me look bad. You need to sit down."

She continued to excel, refusing to let his negativity dim her light. But his resentment grew, festering into a raw, ugly thing. "Does it?" he hissed, his voice laced with contempt. "I'm tired of you trying to be a show-off at church. You're making me look bad. You need to sit down."

What? The word echoed in my mind, a raw, incredulous sound. Obedient to God? Embarrassing him? The disconnect was jarring, a stark illustration of his controlling nature.

Denise felt shattered, her confidence ripped to shreds. From that moment on, she declined every ministry opportunity, hoping to appease him. But his dissatisfaction only morphed, finding new targets. He began to criticize her appearance, her natural hair. "Why do you think Madam C.J. Walker invented the hot comb?" he sneered, his words a calculated blow to her self-esteem.

She was crushed, her spirit broken, her identity eroded. And as she spoke, I saw myself in her pain, the shared experience a chilling reminder that I was not alone in my suffering. The bathroom floor was a crowded space, filled with women silenced, broken, and struggling to find their voices.

What's happening to my soulmate?" Denise asked, her voice a raw whisper. "He was sweet, supportive, understanding. Now, it's like he's made a complete U-turn."

In that moment, the weight of the church announcement, the sting of my own betrayal, faded into the background. Denise's pain was a raw, gaping wound, demanding attention. She wasn't done, the floodgates of her anguish still wide open.

"He started criticizing everything," she continued, her voice trembling. "My clothes, my dates, everything was wrong. Too tight, too short, too much." A season of constant criticism, a slow erosion of her self-worth.

She tried to adapt, to appease him. She increased her prayer life, desperately seeking strength. She abandoned her natural hair, the symbol of her identity, and adopted long, conservative dresses. She became a shadow of herself, a ghost of the vibrant woman he'd once loved.

And when he saw her changing, conforming to his image, he mocked her. "Are you going through menopause?" he sneered, his words a calculated blow.

God, give me guidance, she prayed, the words a desperate plea. What has become of this man?

She tried a different tactic, becoming his biggest cheerleader, celebrating his accomplishments, showering him with praise. She craved reciprocation, a moment of recognition, but it never came.

She clung to the belief that he loved her, that the proposal was imminent. Christmas, she thought, the word a fragile hope. But the months stretched on, two years of waiting, of diminishing returns, and the promise remained unfulfilled.

I was speechless, the weight of her story pressing down on me. My friend, the strong, vibrant Denise, was broken, a shadow of her former self, kneeling on the metaphorical bathroom floor. How can I help her?

She began to sob, her body shaking with the force of her grief. "I'm tired of praying," she confessed, the words a raw, honest admission of her exhaustion.

I know that feeling, I thought, the words a silent echo of my own despair. But I couldn't wallow in my own pain. I had to offer her a lifeline, a sliver of hope.

"Listen to God," I said, my voice hoarse, but firm. "Worship music can help." I knew the power of those melodies, the way they could soothe a wounded soul. "But don't give up on prayer."

My friend was broken, her spirit shattered, but I refused to let her succumb to the darkness. We would find strength together, two women on the bathroom floor, clinging to the fragile hope of healing.

Sleep eluded me. Denise's pain, Terry's manipulative texts—a chaotic swirl of emotions kept me trapped in a cycle of anxious thoughts. He'd texted, feebly attempting to explain the wedding announcement, claiming ignorance of his fiancé's intentions. Sick of him. I wanted to block him, to sever the connection, but a dark, morbid curiosity held me back. Lord, help me.

Then came a text from Lori, my administrative assistant. She needed to talk, first thing in the morning. What now? I thought, a wave of weariness washing over me. I texted back a curt "sure," bracing myself for another emotional storm.

Lori was waiting at my office door, her body trembling, her nails gnawed to the meat. I rushed her inside, but she collapsed, a heap of raw emotion on the floor. Bathroom floor, my mind screamed, the phrase a chilling echo of my own despair.

I helped her up, but she was inconsolable. "How do you do it?" she sobbed, her voice raw with pain. "How do you keep going?"

She revealed her secret: her husband's infidelity, his abrupt decision to leave, the three children caught in the crossfire. *Why me, God?* I thought, a surge of resentment battling with a reluctant empathy. She talked about me. The memory of her gossip, her judgmental whispers, was a bitter taste in my mouth. Satan's knocking on her door, and she can't handle it.

But I pushed aside my own bitterness, forcing myself to be present. Lori's pain was a raw, gaping wound, demanding attention.

She recounted the confrontation, the moment she caught them together, the blind rage that had driven her to attempt vehicular homicide. She spoke of threats, of packing bags, of a husband leaving on a "business trip." And then, she showed me the gun.

Jesus. I thought, my heart pounding. She's crazier than I am.

I tried to reason with her, to convince her that her rage was temporary, a symptom of her pain. But she was adamant. "I mean every word," she said, her eyes blazing with a chilling intensity.

Blank sheet of paper. I felt that emptiness again, that sense of being utterly unprepared. I need to help her.

"Do you want your husband back?" I asked, my voice soft.

"Yes," she sobbed, collapsing to the floor once more.

This is horrible, I thought, the weight of her pain pressing down on me. This is what my friend went through with me.

I let her cry, offering a silent, understanding presence. When she finally regained her composure, I told her the truth: "You're going to have to fight for him. And you're going to have to forgive him."

She looked at me, her eyes filled with a desperate plea. "Counsel me," she begged. "Please."

The request caught me off guard. I'd almost forgotten my profession, lost in the chaos of my own emotional turmoil. "Did you know he was cheating?" she asked, her voice laced with suspicion.

"My life was full," I replied, my voice flat. "The only person I could keep up with was me."

Her next question, a desperate plea for validation, was a chilling echo of my own insecurities. "What are people going to say?"

And without thinking, the words spilled out, a raw, unfiltered truth. "The same things you guys said about me." Oops. The words hung in the air, a stark reminder of the corrosive power of gossip, and the shared vulnerability that bound us together.

"Don't apologize," I said, my voice firm, cutting through her self-recrimination. "We were both wrong. But we're not going to worry about what others say. When Satan knocks on their door, they'll see how strong they really are."

Where are these words coming from? I wondered, a chilling realization of my own fractured state. I'm just as messed up as she is. But I pushed the thought aside, focusing on Lori's raw, undeniable pain.

I saw the physical toll it had taken: the rapid weight loss, the gaunt face, the clothes hanging loosely, held together by safety pins. This is bad. Very bad.

The office phone rang, one of the therapists was looking for Lori. I told her to pull herself together, to remember that "the battle is not hers, it's the Lord's." She emerged from the restroom, her face a carefully constructed mask. The bathroom floor face, I recognized, the hollow-eyed facade of forced composure.

After she left, I broke down, the sobs racking my body, a release of the pent-up pain for both of us.

My best friend called, her voice laced with concern. She'd seen Denise at the grocery store. "She looks different," she said, her voice hesitant. "Sad."

She looks like me, I thought, but kept the thought to myself.

I called Denise, checking in. She was feeling optimistic, her voice bright. Her "soulmate" had invited her for a weekend with his family. This is good, I thought, a fragile hope blossoming.

Denise called back, her voice bubbling with excitement. The weekend had been perfect, a rekindling of their lost connection. "He's back," she declared, her voice filled with a triumphant joy. "Hallelujah! He asked me to brunch!"

He'd asked her to brunch, a date at their favorite restaurant.

Maybe he'll propose, I thought, a surge of vicarious excitement.

But the brunch was a cruel charade. He held her hand, started rubbing it, spoke of their relationship, of her impact on his life. This is it, she thought, her heart pounding, a nervous excitement building. "Oh my God, this is the day I am so nervous," she thought to herself. She even thought about going to the restroom but was too afraid to interrupt the moment.

Then came the devastating blow. "We've been together for almost two years now," he said, his voice flat, devoid of emotion. "And I don't see it going anywhere."

What? The word echoed in her mind, a raw, incredulous sound.

He continued, his words a calculated act of cruelty. "I don't want to hold you back from your goals. I want you to follow your dreams. I'm not ready for marriage. And I want to date other people."

You want to do what?

Date other people? The words were a slap in the face, a brutal rejection of their shared history.

"Are you crazy?" Denise hissed, her voice trembling with rage. "Two years of my life, and you want me to see how the dating world is?"

She pulled her hand away, the gesture a violent severing of their connection. Then, in a moment of raw, unadulterated fury, she pulled her seat from the table and threw the glass of water in his face.

She staggered out of the restaurant, her legs failing her. She barely made it to the bathroom before collapsing, the sound of her fall a loud, echoing thud. The bathroom floor, once a metaphor, was now a cold, hard reality.

The bathroom became a revolving door of concerned faces.

Ladies, their voices laced with pity and worry, asked if she was alright. One of them alerted the manager, who rushed in, his eyes wide with alarm. He asked if an ambulance was needed.

Denise, her voice hoarse and trembling, pleaded for a moment of privacy. "I just need to pull myself together," she whispered. "I'll leave shortly."

The manager, unsure what to do, but sensing the depth of her distress, reluctantly agreed. He placed an "Out of Order" sign on the bathroom door, creating a temporary sanctuary.

Three hours. Three hours she remained there, a prisoner of her own shattered heart. The manager, his concern growing, periodically brought her water, his eyes filled with a silent, unspoken question.

Finally, she emerged, her head held high, a mask of composure plastered over her ravaged features. She thanked the manager, her voice steady, but her eyes betrayed the storm raging within. He stared at her, incredulous. This was the same woman who had been sprawled on the bathroom floor?

Denise drove home in a daze, the world a blur of pain and disbelief. Her cell phone buzzed incessantly, a relentless barrage of calls and texts from "Mr. Soulmate." Why is he calling? she thought, her blood boiling. He's caused enough pain for one day.

She reached her apartment, the silence amplifying the chaos within her. She longed to call her family, but the thought of explaining, of reliving the humiliation, was unbearable. She needed a confidante, someone who understood the raw, unfiltered pain.

She called me. "Can you come over? Immediately," she pleaded, her voice thick with tears. "I need someone I can get naked with."

I arrived to find her a whirlwind of raw emotion, steam practically radiating from her ears. She was a mess, a chaotic blend of rage and despair. She paced, she yelled, she threw objects, the apartment becoming a physical manifestation of her shattered heart.

And through it all, she talked, her words a torrent of pain, a raw, unfiltered outpouring of her broken soul. I didn't interrupt. I didn't offer platitudes or empty reassurances. I simply listened, my heart breaking for her, and prayed, silently, fervently, for a strength we both desperately needed.

The bathroom floor syndrome had taken root, its insidious tendrils wrapping around Denise's soul. She cried herself to sleep, her body wracked with sobs. In the dead of night, she'd jolt awake, her voice a raw, desperate plea: "Why me? Why me?"

The first two weeks were a living hell, a relentless cycle of pain and disbelief. At work, she methodically removed her soulmate's photos from her desk, one by one, a silent act of severance. She moved through her days like a ghost, a hollow shell of her former self. "I'm numb," she told me, her voice flat, devoid of emotion.

She'd stopped attending church, a stark departure from her usual devotion. The pastor and co-pastor, concerned by her absence, reached out, their voices laced with worry. But she offered vague excuses, her words a thin veil over the raw wound beneath. They knew she wasn't telling the truth, but respected her silence.

Each day, she retreated into her apartment, a self-imposed prison. She withdrew from social gatherings, from family, claiming a need for solitude. This is my season alone, she'd say, her voice hollow. But her isolation was a dangerous silence, a breeding ground for despair. I watched, my own anxiety growing, as she existed, not lived.

Then, one day, she called, her voice a flicker of her old self. "I'm feeling like me again," she declared. "I'm going to church."

Church? I thought, my heart pounding. Their church? "Are you sure?" I asked, my voice laced with concern.

"It's my church too," she replied, her voice firm. "I'm a big girl."

Sunday arrived, and I was a nervous wreck. Was he there? How would she react? I waited for her call, for a text, anything.

Then, it came. "Church 911." The cryptic message sent a jolt of panic through me. Oh my God, what happened?

I called, but she didn't answer. I texted, but there was no response. My anxiety spiraled, each unanswered call, each ignored text, a hammer blow to my fragile composure. I called and texted a hundred times, before she finally responded.

"He's here," she texted, her words laced with a chilling calm. "Sitting next to another sister."

Then, the final, devastating detail. "When I walked around the altar to pay my tithes and offering, they both looked at me like I was crazy for coming to church."

A surge of rage, cold and violent, washed over me. "I'm going to get them both," she texted, her words a chilling promise.

"Denise, please," I pleaded, my voice trembling. "Don't do anything crazy."

"Call me crazy," she replied, her words a dark, ominous warning. "Because it's not over."

Do you know," Denise texted, her words seething with rage, "this man had the nerve to call, and when I didn't answer, he texted, telling me not to come back to church?"

What the hell? The words echoed in my mind, a raw,

incredulous sound. This means war.

"And," she continued, her rage escalating, "he's dating her. The sister who always laughed in my face, who complimented us on how 'perfect' we looked together."

The betrayal was a fresh wound, a brutal reminder of her shattered trust. All the progress she'd made, the fragile steps away from the bathroom floor, crumbled beneath her feet. She was back, flat on her back, an "angry black woman," fueled by a righteous fury.

"How could he do this to me?" she texted, her words a raw, guttural cry.

The next Sunday, she arrived at church, a vision of defiant transformation. Dreadlocks framed her face, a bold statement of her newfound strength. She walked around the altar, where her ex-soulmate stood collecting the offering, and winked at him.

The new woman, his companion, kept her head down. Denise touched her shoulder, her voice dripping with saccharine sweetness. "Smile," she said. "God is good."

The woman jumped, startled, and fled to the bathroom, her face a mask of fear and confusion. Denise, her own rage simmering beneath a veneer of calm, returned to her seat.

But the facade crumbled the moment she left the sanctuary. She rushed home, collapsing onto her bathroom floor, a torrent of tears and screams erupting from her soul. Why me?

Guilt gnawed at her. She knew her actions were vindictive, but the desire for revenge, to inflict the same pain she felt, was overwhelming. "I want to make their lives miserable," she confessed, her voice thick with hatred. "I don't want them to be happy."

She enlisted my help, a reluctant accomplice in her quest for vengeance. "If you see them together outside of church," she asked, her eyes burning with a dark intensity, "what will you do?"

I didn't know. I was just an "angry black woman," caught in the crossfire of her pain.

I tried to reason with her, to pull her back from the precipice, but each attempt was met with a renewed descent into the bathroom floor. *Was I this bad?* I wondered, a chilling realization of my own destructive tendencies.

I suggested she return to our church, a sanctuary away from her tormentors, but she refused. "They won't run me out of my ministry," she declared, her voice laced with defiance. "They'll leave before I do."

Her ex-soulmate, sensing her escalating instability, contacted her family, urging them to seek help for Denise. "He thinks I'm losing it," she texted, her rage reaching a fever pitch. "He'll see who's losing it."

Sunday arrived, and he was a no-show. A coward, she thought, her anger boiling over. She drove to his house, pounding on the door, her voice escalating into a furious roar.

The neighbors emerged, their faces etched with concern. "Is everything alright?" they asked.

"No!" she screamed, her voice raw with pain and fury. "Everything is not alright! I'm tired of pretending!"

As they retreated into their homes, she snapped. A split-second of madness. She grabbed a chair from his porch and hurled it at his car window, the shattering glass a violent punctuation mark to her rage. Police cars swarmed the street, sirens wailing.

She was taken into custody, released after paying for the damages. Horrible, she thought, a wave of shame washing over her. What have I done?

Emotionally drained and physically ill, she retreated from church for two weeks. When she finally returned, the congregation's stares were a mix of judgment and morbid curiosity.

But she held her head high, focusing on the sermon, clinging to the fragile hope of healing. A work in progress, she thought, the words a mantra, a promise of a future beyond the bathroom floor.

8

Losing It

I was losing it. Denise and Lori were unraveling, their lives a chaotic mess, and I was dangerously close to joining them. Terry continued to call and text, each unanswered plea a subtle erosion of my resolve. I wanted to talk to him, needed to talk to him, to be back in his orbit, regardless of the wreckage he'd left behind. The walls were closing in, and I needed an escape, a lifeline. I called my bestie, the only constant in my increasingly turbulent world, and asked her to dinner.

I promised myself, a desperate, fragile vow, that Terry's name wouldn't cross my lips. I knew she was weary of my self-destructive spiral, but she was the only one who saw me, truly saw me, stripped bare of my defenses. We settled into a seafood restaurant, the familiar comfort a temporary reprieve from the storm raging within. I wanted to talk about Terry, the ache a constant, gnawing presence, but I forced a smile. Girl's night, I reminded myself, a desperate attempt to cling to normalcy.

We laughed, we talked, we pretended, but the tension was a tangible thing, a silent acknowledgment of the unspoken. Then, I saw her. A member from church. Please, no, I thought, a wave of dread washing over me. Not tonight.

"She's on the bathroom floor," I said to my bestie, my voice low, a chilling observation.

She looked at me, her eyes filled with a mixture of confusion and exasperation. "What are you talking about?"

"Look at her," I said, gesturing subtly. "The fake smile, the fake hair, the clothes, the lashes… the face. She's transformed. She never looked like this before. She's hurting."

"Terry's got you thinking crazy," she retorted, her voice sharp, a cutting accusation.

The mention of his name was like a raw wound, tearing open the fragile peace we'd constructed. "Since you brought him up," I said, my voice trembling, "I need to tell you something."

I confessed, the words spilling out in a rush of guilt and shame. "He's been here. To my house."

Her reaction was a mixture of hurt and anger, her voice laced with disbelief. "Why? Why would you let him? He's a user. You've forgotten how to love yourself."

"Don't say that," I whispered, tears pricking my eyes, the raw truth of her words cutting deep.

"But it's true!" she insisted, her voice rising. "You need to choose yourself."

I couldn't speak, the weight of my shame crushing me. I had lost myself, completely and utterly. The tears that fell were not the raw, desperate sobs of the bathroom floor, but tears of a painful awakening. He'll keep using me, I thought, the realization a cold, hard truth. As long as I let him.

My phone buzzed incessantly, a chorus of desperate calls and texts. Terry, Lori, Denise—all demanding my attention, pulling me further into the chaos. Seven missed calls from Terry alone.

"What are you going to do?" my bestie asked, her voice laced with a weary resignation.

"I'm not going to respond," I said, my voice barely a whisper, a fragile declaration of intent.

She looked at me, her eyes filled with a skeptical disbelief that cut me deeper than any insult. "Sure," she said, her voice flat.

The lack of trust, the unspoken accusation, was a sharp, agonizing pain. "I need to call Denise and Lori back," I said, my voice trembling, trying to justify my actions.

"It's your life," she replied, her voice distant, a chilling reminder of the growing chasm between us. The unspoken words hung heavy in the air: You're making a mistake.

I left my car behind, driving her vehicle, the weight of her desperation a heavy, suffocating presence in the confined space. I was spiraling and I was bringing her with me.

We left the restaurant, the strained silence between us a heavy, unspoken burden. I called Denise first, but she didn't answer, so I texted, asking her to call when she had a moment. Before I could even put my phone away, Lori was calling, her voice a frantic, hysterical shriek. Lord, please don't let her have done something crazy.

"Calm down," I pleaded, my voice trembling, "I can't understand you."

"Come to my house," she sobbed, her words barely coherent. I didn't know where she lived, and I was terrified of what I might find. I told her to stay on the phone, to guide me, to keep me from walking into a potential disaster.

She managed to give me her address, a secluded neighborhood of sprawling, expensive homes. "Where are the kids?" I asked, my voice tight.

"With my parents," she replied, her voice thick with tears.

I arrived to find her waiting at the door, her hands shaking, clutching a stack of papers. Divorce papers. Wow. I was trapped, obligated to help, but dread coiled in my stomach.

"I want my marriage to work," she cried, her voice raw with desperation. "We have three children."

"Where is he?" I asked, my voice low, bracing myself for the answer.

"With her," she spat, her voice laced with venom. "The woman I caught him with."

She confessed to going to the mistress's house and slashing both her husband's and the mistress's tires, her voice devoid of remorse. "They deserve it," she hissed.

"You could go to jail," I said, my voice shaking.

"I don't care," she replied, her eyes burning with a cold, terrifying rage. "They can't prove it was me."

Her husband has to know she slashed his tires and his mistress tires, I thought, a wave of dread washing over me. This could escalate quickly.

The betrayal cut deep. They had been together since childhood, built a life together, a beautiful home. But what seemed to shatter her was the custody battle, the threat of losing her children, her home.

"No other woman will live in a house I helped build," she snarled, her voice a low, menacing growl. "We had nothing when we got married. I worked three and four jobs to put him through medical school. Now he thinks he can take everything?"

"I should have killed them both," she muttered, her voice laced with a chilling calm.

"Don't say that," I pleaded, my voice trembling. "Don't say that to anyone."

"I don't care," she replied, her eyes glazed with a terrifying detachment. "I'm out of control."

"Where's the gun?" I asked, my voice barely a whisper. "I need to take it."

She handed it over, the weight of the loaded weapon heavy in my hand. Done, I thought, my heart pounding. She's completely done.

I had to get her out of there, away from the scene, before the police arrived. "Pack some clothes," I said, my voice firm, masking my fear. "You're staying with me."

She obeyed, moving like a puppet, her tears a constant, silent stream. This is going to be a long night.

"We're taking your car," I said, my voice urgent. "If the police come, we can say you were out of town."

I left my car behind, driving her vehicle, the weight of her desperation a heavy, suffocating presence in the confined space. I was spiraling and I was bringing her with me.

As we pulled up to the house, I saw a figure on my porch. Oh hell, I know better. Terry. Oh no. Lori looked at me, her eyes filled with a silent, questioning dread. "What's going on with you and Terry?" she asked, her voice tight.

We got out of the car, the air thick with unspoken tension. The first words out of his mouth were, "Whose car are you driving?" Are you serious? I thought, my anger simmering.

I opened the door, ushering Lori inside. "Stay outside," I told Terry, my voice flat, devoid of emotion.

He looked at me, incredulous. "Stay outside?"

"Yes," I replied, my voice firm. "Stay outside."

I got Lori settled, a whirlwind of fear and exhaustion, then turned back to face Terry. This is it, I thought, bracing myself for the inevitable confrontation.

"Where have you been?" he demanded, his voice laced with

resentment. "Why haven't you returned my calls?"

My mouth hung open, a silent testament to my disbelief. The audacity. I didn't answer, just stared at him, my eyes filled with a cold, unwavering anger. "What do you want, Terry?"

"I want you," he said, his voice softening, a dangerous, seductive whisper. "I've always wanted you. Life is just... complicated."

Complicated? I thought, a bitter laugh rising in my throat. "You've made my life a living hell," I retorted, my voice laced with venom.

He tried to pull me close, but I recoiled, the physical contact a violation. "Not today," I hissed. "I'm not falling for your lies. I have Lori on the bathroom floor, and I'm not joining her there tonight."

"Can I hold you?" he pleaded, his voice thick with longing. "I miss your smell, your touch."

"No," I said, my voice firm, unwavering. "If you have nothing else to say, you can leave." Come through, Jesus, I thought, a silent prayer for strength.

He recoiled, his eyes filled with a wounded pride. "You don't need me," he said, his voice laced with a bitter accusation. "You never needed me."

Are you serious? I thought, my anger reaching a boiling point.

He continued, his voice rising in self-justification. "My fiancé needs me. She has time for me. You're always working. You never had time."

The words were a twisted mockery of the truth. I don't believe what I'm hearing.

I let him rant, his words a pathetic attempt to rewrite our history. When he finally stopped, I looked at him, my eyes filled with a cold, unwavering clarity. "So," I said, my voice low, "you didn't want an independent woman. You wanted a dependent one."

"You always twist my words," he retorted, his voice laced with frustration. "You don't understand."

"How am I twisting facts, Terry?" I asked, my voice dangerously calm. "Do you want me?"

You know I want you, I thought, the old longing a dangerous, familiar ache. But I kept the words locked inside, a silent battleground of conflicting desires.

I didn't answer, just looked at him, my eyes filled with a cold, unwavering resolve. "It's late," I said, my voice flat. "I need to check on my guest."

He tried to kiss me, a desperate, final attempt to reclaim what he'd lost. I pulled away, the rejection a sharp, decisive act.

He was stunned, his eyes filled with a mixture of confusion and hurt. Yes, be stunned, I thought, the anger a cold, hard knot in my stomach. I'm tired of laying on the bathroom floor.

I turned and walked away, closing the door behind me, the sound a final, decisive act of severance. I stood there, my back against the door, tears streaming down my face. I closed the door on him.

Pull yourself together, I thought, wiping away the tears. Lori didn't need to see me like this. The bathroom floor isn't big enough for both of us.

Lori was in the bathroom, the sound of the shower a backdrop to her raw, guttural moans. My heart ached, each sound a desperate, animalistic cry. It was the sound of someone broken, someone lost.

Her phone rang incessantly, a relentless intrusion on her grief. Finally, she emerged from the shower, her eyes red and swollen, and answered. It was her mother.

Her husband was looking for her. In a rage. He knew she had slashed his tires, and he was demanding answers. Lori feigned surprise, her voice a brittle mask of innocence. She was "staying with a friend," she told her mother and had "no clue" what he was talking about.

Then, a flicker of vengeful satisfaction. "Whoever did it," she said, her voice laced with a dark, chilling humor, "should have slashed his girlfriend's tires too."

Her mother's silence was telling. She hadn't known about the mistress's tires. Hmmm, Lori thought, a dangerous calculation forming in her mind. *So, you won't tell my mom he's with his mistress.*

Her mother warned her to stay away, to avoid her husband's wrath. He was threatening to call the police. Lori asked about her children, her voice trembling. She planned to pick them up the next evening.

Her mother relayed her husband's demand for their location, his anger escalating. She told him they were with Lori's sister.

"I have to go," Lori said, her voice strained. "I love you."

As soon as she hung up, the mask slipped. "I'm going to kill them," she hissed, her voice a low, venomous growl. "Both of them."

"Give me my gun back," she demanded, her eyes burning with a terrifying intensity.

I refused, my hands tightening around the weapon. Instead, I tried to reach her, to pull her back from the precipice. I spoke of forgiveness, of healing, of finding strength in the midst of pain. I ministered to her soul, my words a desperate attempt to build a fragile bridge across the chasm of her despair.

But as I spoke, I realized I was also ministering to myself. My own wounds, my own anger, my own fear, echoed in her pain. We were both on the bathroom floor, clinging to the fragile hope of redemption.

I gave her three scriptures to meditate on, words that flowed from me tonight with a surprising ease, considering I hadn't opened my Bible in months. We talked about:

- Psalm 9:9-10: "The Lord is a refuge for the oppressed, a stronghold in times of trouble. Those who know your name trust in you, for you, Lord, have never forsaken those who seek you." I told her that God promised us victory over evil, that He heard us, protected us. That even when victory seemed distant, it would come, in His time, not ours.
- Psalm 32:7-8: "You are my hiding place; you will protect me from trouble and surround me with songs of deliverance. I will instruct you and teach you in the way you should go; I will counsel you with my loving eye on you." I explained that God would shield us from trouble, but we had to approach Him with clean hands and a pure heart.
- Joshua 1:9: "Have I not commanded you? Be strong and courageous. Do not be afraid; do not be discouraged, for the Lord your God will be with you wherever you 1 go." Trust in God, I told her. He is our source.

I can't believe we're having this conversation, I thought, a wave of surrealism washing over me. This is the same woman who gossiped about Terry, who laughed at my pain. And now, she was in my house, seeking solace. Only God.

Lori looked at me, her eyes filled with a raw, vulnerable honesty. "I owe you an apology," she said, her voice trembling.

97

My face registered a bewildered surprise. "An apology?"

"I talked about your relationship with Terry," she confessed, her voice thick with shame. "To the staff. I didn't understand what you were going through. Will you forgive me?"

God, you have a strange sense of humor, I thought, a bitter laugh rising in my throat. This woman is reading my mind. "Apology accepted," I said, my voice weary. "We need to get some sleep. Church tomorrow."

Lori began to cry, a release of pent-up pain. "It's normal," I said, my voice soft. "Don't let anyone tell you otherwise. You'll have moments like this for a while."

Lord, I've ministered to her, but I'm feeling so weak, I thought, a wave of vulnerability washing over me. One moment, I felt strong, courageous, a vessel of Your word. The next, I was a fragile, broken thing.

I didn't let Terry in, I thought, the realization a mixture of triumph and fear. I prayed for this moment, and I closed the door. Had I finally found my strength, or had I made a terrible mistake? What if I've messed up for good?

Exhaustion pulled at me, a heavy, insistent weight. I need sleep, I thought, the words a desperate plea. It's late.

I finally drifted into a fitful sleep, only to be jolted awake by the insistent buzz of my phone. A dream, I thought, my eyes heavy, my mind still mired in the remnants of sleep. I glanced at the clock: 3:00 AM. No one calls at 3:00 AM.

Then, the knocking started, a persistent, rhythmic pounding that cut through the haze of my sleep. I'm losing it again, I thought, a wave of panic washing over me.

I checked my phone. Denise. Denise? I answered, my voice thick with confusion.

"Open the door," she said, her voice weak, barely a whisper.

"What door?" I asked, my mind still struggling to process the situation.

"Your door," she replied, her voice laced with a desperate urgency.

My door? I thought, my confusion mounting. My car isn't outside. Why is she here? Alone? At this hour?

I opened the door, and she collapsed, falling directly onto the floor, her body limp and lifeless. I struggled to drag her inside, my mind reeling. She was pale, weak, a shadow of her former self.

I stared at her, my mind a chaotic jumble of questions and fears. What do I say? What do I do?

I have one person in the guest room, on the bathroom floor, I thought, my mind racing, one person sprawled in my living room, and me, completely lost, wondering why they all think I have the answers.

Lord, please, I prayed, my voice a silent, desperate plea. Please be with me.

Finally, Denise managed to speak coherently, her voice strained and raw. She explained that her pastor and the First Lady had come to see her. They'd expressed concern, but their timing felt like a cruel joke. "Where were they when he started dating *her*?" Denise asked, her voice laced with bitterness. "When I was still a devoted member? Paying my tithes?"

Why are you here at 3 AM? I wanted to scream, but held my tongue.

The pastors had come bearing devastating news: her ex-soulmate was getting married the very next day, after the church service. They'd suggested she stay away, to avoid a painful surprise.

My heart sank. *This is insane.* "What the hell is going on?" I muttered, my voice thick with disbelief.

Denise was frantic, desperate for answers. "Did they even try to talk to him?" she cried. "How could he just move on like this?"

We were both a mess, tears streaming down our faces, a shared grief for lost love and broken trust. I had no words, no comfort to offer.

Then, Denise dropped another bombshell: she'd had thrown her pastors out of her home. "I told them to leave," she said, her voice trembling with rage, "and never come back. I made it clear that they were no longer welcome in my presence."

"Denise, please," I pleaded, my voice laced with fear. "You didn't...you didn't curse at them, did you?"

"I was polite," she replied, her voice dangerously calm. "But they made it clear: I'm not welcome at church anymore. So, I won't be back. They used me, just like he did."

Why does she keep calling him 'he'? I thought, a flicker of my own denial mirroring hers. *Shut up, you're doing the same thing.*

I tried to reason with her, to explain that the pastors were probably trying to protect her. But she wouldn't listen, her anger a raw, unyielding force.

"I'm crashing the wedding," she declared, her eyes burning with a terrifying resolve.

"No, Denise," I said, my voice firm, laced with a desperate urgency. "You're not going anywhere near that church."

We were both on the floor now, two broken women, trapped in a cycle of pain and denial. *Terry's getting married soon, too,* I thought, a wave of dark, twisted irony washing over me. *Did he come here to stop his own wedding? Is that why he was on my porch?*

Lord, I prayed, my voice a silent, desperate plea. *We are a mess.*

We are lost. Please, just hold us. This night...this day...it has to end.

9

The Altar of Brokenness

N o sleep. Not a wink. Three women, all trapped on the bathroom floor, forced to face the day. We had to go to church. A blessing has to be coming, I told myself, a desperate mantra. There was no other explanation for this simultaneous descent into madness.

Lori, the tire-slasher, Denise, the pastor-evicter, and me, the almost-relapsed lover. We were a walking, talking testament to emotional wreckage. The tension in the car was thick, unspoken. Denise eyed Lori with suspicion, Lori returned the favor, and I sat between them, a silent, seething mess.

We all wore the mask: the "everything is fine" face, a fragile shield against the world. Don't ask me how I am, it screamed. Just don't. We were strong, educated, professional women, reduced to stumbling through life, one shaky step at a time. As we pulled into the parking lot, my phone buzzed. A text from my bestie. Where are you? I ignored it. We were already here, a trio of walking disasters.

Then, we saw him. Terry. Of course. The greeter. Why isn't he with his fiancé? Had he stopped working in the ministry because he thought I would confront her? I plastered on my brightest smile, my blonde hair a defiant flag of my supposed confidence. He'll never know how close I came to breaking last night. Maybe God sent Lori to keep me from him, I thought, a desperate attempt to find meaning in the chaos.

Lori glared at Terry, a silent threat. Don't say a word. Denise, oblivious to the undercurrents, greeted everyone with forced cheer, a desperate attempt to project normalcy. Everyone knows about his wedding, she seemed to scream with her eyes. Everyone!

We made a beeline for the balcony, a desperate escape from the judging eyes below. My bestie's face was a mask of confusion and concern. "What is going on?" her eyes asked.

The choir began to sing, the music a raw, emotional release. I scanned the sanctuary, searching for Terry's fiancé. Where is she? Did they break it off? A flicker of hope, dangerous and foolish, ignited within me. Did I mess up last night? My hands were clammy, my heart pounding with a nervous anticipation.

Then, the choir launched into "Jireh" by Maverick City, the music a tidal wave of emotion. The church was on fire, the spirit palpable. Lori and Denise were swept away, their bodies swaying, their faces contorted with raw emotion. I cried, tears streaming down my face, my own internal battle raging.

But it wasn't the emotional fervor that shocked me. It was something else entirely.

It was the sea of wigs that shocked me. A silent, unspoken acknowledgment of shared vulnerability. The young woman from the restaurant, the one I'd dismissed as 'curly hair,' was laid out on the floor, her wig a disheveled halo around her tear-streaked face. Curly hair women are considered to be dangerous, the thought echoed in my mind, a cruel, judgmental stereotype.

And then I saw it. The sheer number of women, their carefully constructed facades stripped away, their pain laid bare. The realization hit me like a physical blow. We were all broken, all hurting, all desperately seeking solace.

The next thing I knew, I was on the floor, joining Lori and Denise in their raw, uninhibited display of grief. The ushers, always eager to insert themselves into other people's business, descended upon the balcony. "Praise the Lord," one of them declared, her voice laced with a thinly veiled judgment. What a mess.

We finally managed to pull ourselves together as the pastor began his sermon. And he preached. The spirit in the room was palpable, a raw, visceral energy. He even referenced a clip from "The Color Purple," the congregation erupting in laughter at the raw, defiant declaration: "I'm Poor, Black, I May Even Be Ugly, But Dear God, I'M Here! I'M Here!"

The pastor's message was clear: we were worthy, loved, accepted, flaws and all. We just had to believe, to trust in God's process. The tears flowed freely, a collective release of pent-up pain. Then, he called for prayer, and the church erupted. A sea of bodies, a chorus of desperate pleas. He called forward those who had been hurt, those who needed healing.

Curly hair, her sobs uncontrollable, stumbled forward. My bestie touched my arm, her eyes filled with a silent, knowing understanding. She's one of us. Lori and Denise were laid out again, their bodies writhing, their cries echoing through the sanctuary. White sheets covered the floor, a stark reminder of the pain we carried. As the women began to rise, curly hair asked for the microphone. What followed was a raw, unfiltered confession, a testimony that set the church ablaze.

She had planned to end her life after the service, she confessed, her voice trembling. The pastor's quote from "The Color Purple" had been her turning point. She felt unworthy, unloved, rejected. Her partner of three years had left, his words a cruel, devastating blow. I sat in stunned silence, recognizing her pain, her despair. Curly hair, a scientist at the CDC, a successful, accomplished woman, had been on the brink of suicide. Lord, forgive me for judging her last night. The pastor, his voice thick with emotion, called for another prayer line. This time, it was for those contemplating suicide. Denise and Lori, two more successful women, their faces etched with pain, joined the line. And me, I thought, a wave of self-awareness washing over me. I was with them. I didn't want to die, but I couldn't imagine living without Terry.

As I ran down the stairs, desperate for the healing the prayer line offered, he stood there, a solid, immovable presence at the bottom. Terry. A wave of panic, mixed with a dangerous, familiar longing, washed over me.

"Excuse me," I said, my voice trembling, trying to push past him.

"No," he replied, his eyes locking onto mine, his voice low and intense. You have Thirty Seconds, Terry. "Thirty seconds."

Thirty seconds? My heart pounded against my ribs, a frantic drumbeat. Just thirty seconds, a treacherous voice whispered in my mind. Just to hear what he has to say. I knew it was a lie, a dangerous rationalization, but I couldn't seem to stop it.

"Terry, we're at church," I pleaded, my voice laced with desperation. "I'm trying to save myself from you."

"I love you," he said, the words a raw, visceral punch to my gut. The air crackled between us, charged with the weight of our shared history, our unspoken desires. The world around us faded away, the music, the prayers, the raw emotion of the service, all reduced to a distant hum.

My body moved before my mind could process what was happening. My feet carried me forward, an almost involuntary response, a desperate, reckless surrender. I ran towards the altar, towards him, my hand instinctively reaching for his. The craziest thing is, I thought, a whirlwind of confusion and desperate longing swirling within me, I was running with him.

I didn't realize what I was doing, the force that propelled me towards him, until Lori's voice cut through the haze of my desire. "Let go of his hand," she said, her voice firm, a lifeline thrown into my self-made storm.

Help me, Lord, I thought, a silent, desperate plea. Throw all the oil on me. Drench me in your grace. At that moment, I didn't care what anyone thought. I needed the Holy Ghost, and I needed it now.

Terry, his face a mixture of confusion and longing, retreated back towards the door. You should have stayed down here with me, I thought, a bitter irony twisting in my gut. You're just as broken as I am.

The pastor continued to pray, his words a balm to our wounded souls. He urged us to make a difficult decision, to take out our "imaginary scissors" and cut the toxic people and patterns from our lives.

I looked around at the women at the altar, a sea of faces etched with pain. Successful women, strong women, women who appeared to have it all. Yet, here we were, broken, vulnerable, stripped bare of our carefully constructed facades.

These women are me, I realized, the truth hitting me with the force of a physical blow. We hid behind our titles, our accomplishments, our carefully curated images. We defined ourselves by what we did, not by who we were.

And right now, in this moment, I knew who I was. Broken. Hurt. Mad. Frustrated. Alone. And terrified. Terrified of being vulnerable, terrified of being seen, terrified of the emptiness beneath the mask.

I fell to the floor, the weight of my fear crushing me. A primal scream tore from my throat, a desperate cry for deliverance. "Jesus!" I wailed, the name the only anchor in the storm raging within me. "Jesus! Jesus!"

The music swelled, a wave of sound that mirrored the raw emotion in the room. I could hear other women wailing, a chorus of pain and hope, a sound I recognized as the sound of breakthrough, of healing.

Every time I tried to rise, an invisible force pushed me back down, a divine hand pressing against my chest. You are wonderfully made, I heard, a whisper in my soul. You are amazing. You are a child of God. You are beautiful. You are talented. You are my child.

Why are you saying this to me, God? I thought, tears streaming down my face. I know all of this, but I don't believe it. I don't believe that I am any of these things.

Then, I began to speak in tongues, a language I didn't understand, yet somehow knew. God began to whisper more sweet words in my ear, and I felt a sense of calm begin to wash over me. A deep, profound peace, a longing for sleep, for escape. But I knew I couldn't stay on the floor. I had to rise. I had to choose.

As I struggled to rise, Terry extended his hand. A flicker of the old longing, a dangerous temptation, tugged at me. But something had shifted within me, a newfound sense of strength, a determination to move forward. I wanted him to see that I was changed, that the woman who had run to him at the altar was gone.

To my left, Denise and Lori were still on the floor, their cries echoing through the sanctuary. I understood their pain, their desperate need for release. I began to pray for them, for all the women surrounding the altar, a collective plea for healing and deliverance.

The spirit in the room was electric, a raw, untamed energy. The pastor's voice boomed through the microphone, casting out demons, breaking chains. "No weapon formed against me shall prosper!" I repeated the words, a shield against the lingering darkness.

As I finally made my way back to my seat, praising God for the strength I'd found, I saw her. Terry's fiancé. She was crying, her face contorted with grief, and she was moving towards me, her eyes locked on mine.

Okay, God, I thought, a wave of panic washing over me. *She is not about to come up on me.* "No weapon formed against me shall prosper," I repeated, my voice barely a whisper.

Then, she was upon me, her hands grabbing my arm, pulling me into a desperate embrace. She began to apologize, her words a jumbled mess of tears and regret. My body went numb, my mind reeling. *What do I say? What do I do?*

I tried to pull away, to escape the suffocating intensity of her grief, but she clung to me, her sobs growing louder, more desperate. *What is really going on right now? Is this her breakthrough?* God's voice, clear and insistent, echoed in my mind: *Accept her apology.*

God, I am not ready for this, I thought, my internal struggle raging. *I just got off the floor. I am not emotionally equipped.*

I could feel the eyes of the congregation upon us, the awkward silence stretching into an eternity. I wanted to push her away, to retreat into the safety of my own pain, but God's will held me captive. *God, I surrender.*

"I forgive you," I said, the words a strained whisper, a reluctant offering.

And then, she screamed. A raw, guttural sound that ripped through the silence, stopping the service in its tracks. *Oh my God,* I thought, my heart pounding against my ribs. *People are going to think I did something to her. What am I going to do now?*

10

Monday Madness

Don't cry over what I rejected. The blessing is in the release. God's words echoed in my mind, a strange, unsettling comfort. God, what are you saying? I whispered, my voice thick with confusion. "Terry had to reject you", He replied, the voice clear and unwavering, "for me to bless you openly. Yes, my child… I had to remove him from your life because I have something so much greater planned, something you won't believe. I am going to rock your world."

I listened, but understanding remained elusive. It was like trying to decipher a language I only partially knew. I immersed myself in God's word, meditating on His promises, seeking clarity in the midst of my confusion. Gradually, His voice became clearer, more distinct. "It's time to get your life back," He said, a gentle command. "It's time to be free. To laugh, to love, to dance a little."

Fear, a cold, familiar companion, gripped me. I don't feel worthy, God, I confessed, my voice trembling. I don't feel worthy of happiness, of abundance. He led me back to my foundational scripture, Mark 11:22-24, the words resonating with a newfound power:

"Have faith in God," Jesus answered. "Truly I tell you, if anyone says to this mountain, 'Go, throw yourself into the sea,' and does not doubt in their heart but believes that what they say will happen, it will be done for them. Therefore, I tell you, whatever you ask for in prayer, believe that you have received it, and it will be yours."

Believe that you have received it, the words echoed in my mind. Believe. It wasn't just about faith in God's power, but faith in my own worthiness, in my own capacity to receive His blessings. This wasn't just a spiritual detox; it was a soul detox, a shedding of old beliefs and limitations.

I was still grappling with the confusion. I had believed, with every fiber of my being, that Terry was my destined husband. Then, God's voice, sharp and clear, cut through my doubts. You didn't have faith in me. You had faith in Terry. The truth hit me like a physical blow. I had lost sight of the scripture, of the promise of faith in God. Why am I meditating on these scriptures? I wondered, a flicker of impatience rising within me. But I silenced it, reminding myself to trust, to listen.

I called my bestie, sharing God's revelation. Her reaction was a mix of amazement and relief. "I thought you were healing," she said, her voice laced with concern.

"I am," I replied, a newfound determination in my voice. "I'm tired of the bathroom floor.

I'm ready to live, laugh, and dance."

She erupted in a joyous shout, repeating my words like a mantra. "I'm ready for you to have your life back!"

"What do you mean?" I asked, a flicker of defensiveness in my voice.

"Go look in the mirror," she said, her voice firm.

What? I thought, but I obeyed.

The reflection staring back at me was a stranger. Forty pounds heavier, my skin darker, the 360 WIG a desperate attempt to hide the truth. I barely recognized myself. I was still trying to camouflage my life, I realized, a wave of shame washing over me.

The urge to break down, to retreat into the familiar comfort of my pain, was overwhelming. But then, a gentle voice, a sweet spirit, whispered, it's time to detox. It's time to cleanse your soul. Oh my God, I thought, the weight of my denial crushing me. Who is this woman in the mirror? A surge of determination filled me. It's time for change. It's time to make a difference. And it's going to be good. A wave of positive energy washed over me, a feeling of lightness, of liberation.

"Thank you," I said to my bestie, my voice thick with emotion. "Thank you for letting me get NAKED with you."

We both cried, tears of release, of hope, of a shared journey towards healing. "Faith moves forward," I heard God say, the words a powerful affirmation.

And I knew, with unwavering certainty, that I was going to move forward. The first step was a physical and spiritual cleansing. I embraced a diet of vegetables and fruits, committed to daily exercise. I felt my body lighten, my energy surge. I laughed more, smiled more.

People noticed the change. The joy radiating from within, the subtle shift in my skin tone, a reflection of the inner transformation. A new beginning, I thought, a sense of wonder and anticipation filling my soul. A new me.

It was a Marvelous Monday, a stark contrast to the chaos of the previous week. I walked into the office, my steps lighter, my spirit brighter. Lori was at her desk, her eyes scanning me from head to toe. "Do you like what you're looking at?" I asked, a playful smile tugging at my lips. She grinned, a genuine, joyful expression. "I love what I'm looking at! You look amazing!" She reached out, her fingers tracing the texture of my hair. "Is this your hair? It's beautiful!"

I nodded, a sense of quiet pride filling me. The compliments, the genuine happiness in her eyes, felt like a validation of my transformation. The laughter drew our colleagues out of their offices, curious about the commotion. They stared at me, their expressions a mix of surprise and admiration. "Who are you?" one of them asked, their tone laced with disbelief. Was I really that unrecognizable?

They commented on my newfound happiness, the radiant glow that seemed to emanate from within. But, as always, there was one who couldn't resist dredging up the past. One of the counselors, her voice dripping with thinly veiled judgment, recounted the events of the previous week, her words painting a vivid picture of my emotional breakdown, of Lori and me laid out on the floor in the spirit.

Lori, her face flushed with shame, walked out of the office. The other colleagues exchanged uncomfortable glances. "What did I say?" the counselor asked, her voice laced with false innocence. I looked at her, my gaze steady. "When Satan knocks on your door," I said, my voice calm but firm, "how will you handle the storm?" The office fell silent. We all retreated to our respective spaces.

Lori came to my office, her eyes filled with a raw, vulnerable pain. She thanked me for being there, for pulling her back from the edge. Then, the tears came, silent and uncontrollable, a release of pent-up grief. I recognized the pain, the desperate need for catharsis. I gave her the space she needed, a silent acknowledgment of our shared humanity.

When she finally regained her composure, she apologized for her past behavior, for the harsh words spoken during my own vulnerable moment. "We've moved past that," I said, my voice gentle but firm. "But you need to get off the bathroom floor."

She confessed that her husband still hadn't returned home. She was lying to her children, telling them he was away on a conference. She showed me the unanswered texts, the desperate pleas for contact. She was contemplating going to his workplace, or worse, to his mistress's house. I urged her to avoid the latter, but I couldn't deny the logic of confronting him at his job.

"Don't make a scene," I cautioned. "He'll call the police, especially after the tire incident."

She hugged me, a tight, desperate embrace. "Thank you," she whispered, her voice thick with emotion. "Thank you for everything."

As I sat at my desk, the echoes of the weekend's spiritual upheaval still resonating within me, I began to unpack the layers of revelation. I was being 'plucked,' I realized, like the delicate work of shaping a lace-front wig. God was meticulously removing the excess, the artificiality, revealing the natural hairline of my soul. The lies I'd believed, the self-doubt that had festered for so long, were being stripped away, replaced with the undeniable truth: I was loved.

Tears, a cleansing river, flowed freely. Loved by the highest priest, I whispered, the words a balm to my wounded spirit. Loved by Jesus. The realization was both overwhelming and liberating. I had spent so long seeking validation in external sources, in titles and relationships, that I had lost sight of my inherent worth.

A strange numbness settled over me, a stillness that bordered on fear. But God's voice, a gentle reassurance, calmed my anxieties. "Be still, "He whispered." I have you. I have heard your cry." You've heard a lot of crying, I thought, a wry smile touching my lips. I had reached a point where tears seemed to have run dry, yet here they were, flowing freely, a testament to the depths of my healing.

I immersed myself in work, a familiar refuge. The hours blurred, the clock ticking unnoticed. It was after 2:00 PM, and I'd skipped lunch. A sharp knock on my door, followed by its immediate opening, startled me. My boss stood there, her face etched with concern.

"Have you seen Lori?" she asked, her voice tight.

"Earlier," I replied, a knot of dread forming in my stomach.

"She hasn't returned from lunch," my boss stated, her eyes searching mine. What has she done? I thought, the question echoing in the sudden silence. I asked if she had tried calling, and she nodded, her expression grim. I wanted to grab my phone, to check for messages, but I hesitated, not wanting to reveal my growing anxiety.

My boss lingered, her gaze fixed on my hair. "That wig looks really good on you," she commented, a jarringly casual observation in the midst of the tension. "It's not a wig," I corrected her, a flicker of irritation mixing with my concern. "It's my hair." The casual comment felt like a reminder of how much I had changed, and how much others had noticed. "Oh," she said, a moment of awkward silence, and then she left.

I grabbed my purse, my hands trembling slightly. What has happened to Lori? I pulled out my phone. Thirteen missed calls from Lori. My heart pounded against my ribs. A text message, stark and terrifying, confirmed my worst fears: *Pick me up from* *city jail. Bond is $150,000.*

Lord, what has she done? I thought, my mind reeling. I sped through red lights, the city blurring around me, my nerves stretched taut. At the city jail, Lori stood before me, her hands wrapped in thick, white gauze. The sight sent a chill through me.

"What happened?" I demanded, my voice tight with fear and concern.

Her story unfolded in a torrent of rage and grief. She had gone to her husband's practice, only to be met with a cold, dismissive receptionist and the threat of police intervention.

"How dare he?" she screamed, her voice raw with fury. "I helped build that practice! He can't just shut me out!"

She had lost control, she confessed, smashing his office window, a desperate act of defiance.

"He's trying to trap you," I said, my voice urgent. "He'll use this against you. He'll say you're unstable. He'll take the kids."

She erupted, her rage a terrifying force. I pulled the car over, unable to drive through her storm of pain. She cried, she screamed, her eyes filled with a dark, desperate energy.

Finally, after what felt like an eternity, I managed to calm her down, my voice a soothing balm against her fury. "How are you going to explain four hours late from lunch to the boss?" I asked, a grim reminder of the practical consequences of her actions.

Lori, her voice trembling, pleaded, "You have to help me. What am I going to do?"

"You're going to get it together," I said, my voice firm, though my heart ached for her. "You have a lot to think about."

She called her boss, fabricating an accident, a cut hand, a promise to return tomorrow. I shook my head, praying she wouldn't dig herself deeper.

Then, we went to retrieve her car from her husband's office. It was gone, towed. Oh God. The rage returned, a dark, dangerous energy. I steered her into the car, pulling away from his office on two wheels.

At the towing company, her credit card was declined. Her husband had frozen her accounts. This is getting uglier by the moment. It was a struggle to keep her calm, to suppress the urge to unleash my own fury. I paid to release her car, the weight of her desperation heavy on my shoulders.

Back at her house, her children ran towards her, their faces filled with worry. "We saw Daddy in a car with a lady!" To my surprise, she remained composed, brushing it off, asking about their school day. Her youngest child noticed her bandaged hand, and she offered a vague explanation about a work accident.

As I was about to leave, she begged me to stay. "I need a friend."

Her children, sensing the tension, asked to use their cell phone. The oldest called his father, confronting him about the woman in the car.

"It's a coworker," he lied, promising to be home soon.

This is going to be a long day, I thought. Marvelous Monday had morphed into Monday Madness. I warned Lori to keep her composure, especially if her husband showed up. Her children didn't need to witness her unraveling. And then, he arrived, opening the door as if nothing were amiss. He gathered the children in the family room, announcing a temporary separation, citing "differences." The children were confused, Lori's face a mask of pain. The oldest son, his voice hard, asked bluntly, "Are you getting a divorce?" His father evaded the question, offering vague assurances. I wanted to scream, to demand he tell them the truth.

He left, leaving behind a trail of broken promises and shattered illusions. Lori, her voice tight, demanded his credit cards, one for the children, a reminder to pay the mortgage and utilities.

The oldest son, his eyes filled with a painful understanding, announced he knew what was happening. The youngest cried for her daddy. Lori, her voice strained, reassured them, her composure a fragile facade.

He left, and Lori thanked me, her eyes filled with an unbearable sadness. Then, I noticed the curly wig. No more, I wanted to say, but I just smiled.

I helped her get the children ready for bed, and as I was about to leave, she collapsed, a broken heap on the bathroom floor, her cries echoing my own past pain.

On my drive home, my phone rang. Denise, her voice a whirlwind of anger and hurt. She was meeting her ex, the one who had just gotten married, for lunch tomorrow. "He sent me pictures of the wedding," she said, her voice trembling. "It was everything we planned."

Then, a text from him, paragraphs of apologies, a plea for friendship, an invitation to lunch. "He wants to talk about getting back together," she said, her voice filled with a desperate hope. I wanted to shake her, to scream at her to see the manipulation. But I knew she wouldn't listen.

"Go," I said, my voice flat. "Find out what he has to say."

She asked if she could stay the night at my place. She said she was too emotionally drained to drive, and she needed to be "prepared" for her lunch date. The thought of her driving in her current state was frightening, so I agreed.

As she slept, I retreated to my room, the tears flowing freely, a release of the day's accumulated stress. But beneath the sadness, a flicker of joy, a sense of liberation.

"My God, my God, you are awesome," I whispered, the words a prayer of gratitude.

I slept soundly, and the next morning, I found a note from Denise. She had left for her lunch date, promising to call later.

11

Dummy Down

Denise's call was jarringly cheerful. Please don't tell me you're becoming the other woman, I thought, a wave of protective concern washing over me. She wanted to come over after work, bringing dinner, her voice bubbling with excitement about all she had to discuss. I agreed without hesitation. A broken heart could lead you down treacherous paths, and I wouldn't turn away anyone teetering on the edge.

Lori was a ghost today. Her car was in the parking lot, a silent testament to her presence, but her office remained empty. Finally, I found her at her desk, her usual vibrant energy replaced by a heavy stillness. Her 360 wig was pulled up in a tight, severe ponytail, a stark contrast to her usual flowing style. She looked...diminished.

Lost in her own world, she didn't notice me standing in her doorway. "Lori?" I called softly. No response. "Lori?" I tried again, a little louder. She flinched, acting as though she'd been deeply engrossed in her computer screen. When she finally looked up, her eyes were swollen and red-rimmed.

"What's going on?" I asked gently, my heart heavy.

"I don't feel like talking," she mumbled, her gaze fixed on her hands.

I respected her silence, but I left my door ajar, a silent invitation, a beacon in her darkness.

Back in my office, snippets of hushed conversations drifted from the hallway. The police had brought Lori a letter. Curiosity gnawed at me. A letter? After her arrest? After her husband's callous actions? And her silence all day…something felt deeply wrong. The "dummy down" feeling settled in – a sense that something significant was happening beneath the surface that I wasn't privy to, and perhaps Lori was intentionally keeping it that way, playing naive to avoid further scrutiny.

My Bestie's unexpected arrival at the workplace was a welcome burst of sunshine. I ushered her into my office, relieved for a friendly face amidst the lingering tension. She explained she was just passing by, wanting to check on me – a testament to her unwavering thoughtfulness.

As she studied me, a familiar knowing look in her eyes, my heart hitched. *Here it comes,* I thought, bracing for the Terry conversation. But it didn't. Instead, she showered me with compliments, remarking on my clothes, my hair, the newfound clarity in my complexion, the subtle weight loss.

A genuine laugh bubbled up within me, and I recounted my spiritual encounter the previous night, the shift from bathroom-floor despair to joyful thanksgiving. She squeezed my hand, her eyes filled with warmth. "You're going to be okay," she affirmed, urging me to continue meditating on God's word. We shared more laughter, a much-needed balm to my soul.

I mentioned Denise's impending visit, her post-lunch-date debrief, and asked my Bestie to join us. "I might kill her if I'm alone with her," I joked, the underlying seriousness clear. We set a time for later that evening, and I walked her to her car.

Returning to the office, Lori intercepted me, her eyes pleading. The entire office seemed to hold its breath, every door ajar, every ear straining. I ushered her into my office, turning up my gospel music to create a semblance of privacy.

She wordlessly handed me the letter. A restraining order. Her husband was accusing her of stalking. Disbelief and fury warred on her face. "What about the children?" I asked, my voice barely a whisper. He was trying to take them.

The fight seemed to drain out of her, and she sank to her knees, the silent tears beginning to flow again. I knelt beside her, offering a silent prayer for strength and peace. When I finished, a guttural cry ripped from her throat, so loud it echoed through the stunned office.

The office staff surged towards my door, a wave of morbid curiosity. I locked it, the "dummy down" act now a necessary shield. They wouldn't understand. They wouldn't see the raw pain, the desperation of a woman pushed to her breaking point. They would only see the drama.

I yelled through the locked door, "She's sick! We'll be out soon!" But they didn't disperse. I could hear their heavy breathing, their hushed whispers. They were the worst, a nosy, intrusive bunch. It was no wonder they were in this profession – drama seemed to be their lifeblood. The "dummy down" act I had hoped for wasn't working on them; they were too invested in the spectacle.

I helped Lori off the floor, her body limp and heavy with despair, and guided her to the couch in my office. I went to the boss, explaining that Lori had received devastating news and I would keep her with me until she felt stable enough to go home. Our boss, thankfully, was understanding.

In the quiet of my office, a plan began to form. "It's okay to have your moments on the bathroom floor," I told Lori, my voice firm but compassionate, "but now you have to think like him." In the span of an hour, we secured her an attorney and started putting a strategy into motion.

A flicker of anger, a bitter memory of Lori's laughter during my own breakdown, threatened to surface. But God's gentle nudge was immediate: *Not today. Move forward.* It wasn't about my hurt feelings; it was about another woman on the bathroom floor, desperately in need of support.

As the workday ended, Lori, though still fragile, had pulled herself together. I followed her home, a silent promise of support hanging in the air. I couldn't stay long; Denise and my Bestie would be arriving soon.

Finally home, I rushed through a shower, washing away the residue of Lori's pain and the office's suffocating atmosphere. I knew tonight would be another emotional marathon. Denise and my Bestie arrived almost simultaneously, Denise bearing pasta and salad, her face radiating a disconcerting happiness. *Please, please don't tell me you're settling for being the other woman,* I pleaded silently.

As we ate, Denise launched into a giddy recount of her forty-minute drive and "amazing" lunch. She gushed about the wedding's uncanny resemblance to their own meticulously planned nuptials. I listened, forcing myself to remain neutral, though a knot of nausea tightened in my stomach.

He'd told her he'd replicated their wedding plans intentionally, a constant reminder of her. My internal alarm bells screamed. He'd confessed he loved her, admitting his "mistake," and wanted them to...continue being " friends."

My Bestie interjected, her voice laced with concern. "Denise, honey, that sounds like a recipe for more heartbreak."

But Denise was lost in her own narrative, her ears deaf to reason. *He wants you to be his side chick,* I thought, the words a bitter taste in my mouth. "Denise," I finally interrupted, my voice firm, "do you love yourself?"

"Yes, of course, I love myself," she replied, her brow furrowing.

"No," I countered, my gaze unwavering. "You don't love yourself enough to settle for this."

She continued, oblivious, recounting his reasons for marrying his wife. Apparently, the new wife was a good listener, content to let him take the spotlight. He craved control, something Denise, with her strong personality and independence, hadn't allowed. He'd even admitted his insecurity about her higher income, a confession he'd made years ago when she first joined their ministry, feeling overshadowed by her.

So, he's a man riddled with insecurities, I thought, the pieces clicking into place. Denise, blinded by love, was willingly "dummying down," ignoring the glaring red flags, clinging to the crumbs of his affection.

Here we go again. Another powerful woman willingly "dummying down" her brilliance, dimming her light to inflate a man's fragile ego. And this man was married, expecting his side woman to shrink herself, to forget her own worth and belonging. The irony wasn't lost on me. I had walked that same destructive path with Terry. How could I possibly steer Denise away from this cliff edge when I had so recently teetered there myself? The bathroom floor was a lonely, seductive place, and the pull of love, however twisted, made it agonizingly difficult to escape its cold embrace.

My Bestie valiantly tried to reason with Denise, her words falling on deaf ears. Denise was determined, stubbornly clinging to the illusion of a rekindled romance. When we asked about returning to the ministry, her nonchalant "why not?" sent a chill down my spine. This was going to be a messy, painful descent. My Bestie finally fell silent, recognizing the futility of arguing with someone so determined to be blind, so willing to "dummy down" her own truth.

Sunday morning arrived, a fresh start. I surveyed my closet, deliberately bypassing the WIGS. Today was about embracing my natural self, the highlights catching the light, a reflection of the inner radiance I was beginning to feel. My maxi dress, once a comfortable staple, now swam around me. A shock, but a welcome one, a tangible sign of my healing. After a brief search, I found a flattering A-line dress that fit perfectly. I was ready to face my giant.

The church parking lot was overflowing. Running late. As I walked through the doors, there he was. Terry, ushering. My stomach lurched, a familiar wave of anxiety threatening to overwhelm me. *Self-talk, quick self-talk,* I commanded myself. I lifted my chin, my gaze steady, and walked with a newfound confidence. Terry's face registered a flicker of confusion, a silent acknowledgment of the change in me. My stomach was still churning, a desperate plea for a bathroom break, but I refused to let him see my vulnerability. A silent prayer for calm, and miraculously, the bubbling subsided. I could finally focus on the praise and worship, my heart slowly filling with a genuine peace.

Praise and worship resonated deeply within me, the anointing in the room almost tangible. When the pastor called for altar call, I went forward, my prayers a fervent plea for Denise as much as for myself. I felt the weight of every eye on me. Terry stood at the altar, and his fiancé was in the prayer line, a silent tableau of our tangled past.

I caught snippets of whispers from the church mothers, their voices laced with judgment. *She's lost weight. That dress is too revealing.* A sharp retort sprang to my lips, but God's immediate rebuke silenced me.

As I walked away from the altar, Terry's fiancé, tears streaming down her face, reached for me. I embraced her, a gesture of unexpected compassion. She almost collapsed, and security guards moved in, asking me to step away.

I retreated towards my seat, a quiet triumph blossoming in my chest. I wasn't the same woman who had crumbled on this floor months ago. Terry grabbed my arm. This time, I didn't flinch. I stood my ground. "Yes, Terry?"

He seemed taken aback by my composure. "You look nice," he stammered.

"Thank you," I replied, a polite dismissal, and continued to my seat.

Church dismissed, but neither Denise nor my Bestie were there. No missed calls, no texts. I called Bestie, but she didn't answer. Then, Denise's frantic call broke through, her words a jumbled torrent of distress. My Bestie finally got on the line, her voice heavy. She had gone to church with Denise, and it had been a disaster. Her ex had completely ignored her, and church members had questioned her return. The First Lady had even asked her not to come back, citing a desire to avoid drama now that her ex had "moved on."

I was speechless. Denise was on the bathroom floor. I asked Bestie to bring her to my house. The moment Denise walked in, she bolted for the bathroom, the door slamming shut behind her.

"Let her have her moment," I told Bestie, recognizing the

familiar signs. Three hours. That's how long Denise remained in that self-imposed exile, the sounds of her crying and yelling a heartbreaking symphony of pain. I knew that cry. It was the cry of someone who had reached rock bottom, a place where words and comfort offered no solace. Only time, a slow, agonizing process, could begin to lift her from the cold, hard tiles.

Denise was battling the double blow of her ex's callous disregard and the deep wounds of church hurt. For someone who had been a faithful and dedicated member, this rejection must have felt like a profound betrayal. I was so grateful Bestie had been there with her.

There truly is nothing like the bathroom floor. It's a unique kind of agony, a solitary confinement of the soul that no one can fully comprehend unless they've been exiled there themselves. When Satan knocks at your door with the force of heartbreak, prepare for the storm. There is perhaps no greater pain than loving someone with your entire being only to have your heart and your feelings dismissed as if they were nothing. In those moments, you can feel like you've wandered into the pages of the Diagnostic and Statistical Manual of Mental Disorders, Fifth Edition (DSM-5), questioning your own sanity.

That's why having someone you can get NAKED with – someone who sees you in your rawest, most vulnerable state and loves you unconditionally – is a lifeline. That person can be the anchor that prevents you from lashing out and causing further hurt. And knowing Jesus Christ, having that unwavering spiritual foundation, is crucial, even though prayer can feel like an impossible task when you're consumed by the fiery rage of a MADD woman.

But through it all, remember your self-worth. Cling to it fiercely. Never, ever allow anyone to diminish your value or make you believe you are not worthy of love and respect. It is okay to visit the bathroom floor; it's a necessary space for grief and raw honesty. Just don't take up permanent residence there. Because it's on that cold, hard tile that you often confront your true self, stripped bare of pretense. And once you find the strength to rise, Satan trembles, because a woman who has faced her darkness and found her light is a force that can conquer the world.

About the Author

Dr. Saketha Q. Adams is more than an experienced higher education administrator; she is a visionary leader fueled by a deep-seated passion for student success and a profound compassion for the communities she serves. Her professional journey, which began as an Adult Education Instructor, is a compelling testament to her relentless drive and consistent ability to ignite positive change.

Beyond her professional achievements, Saketha has channeled her personal experiences into her powerful book, "On the Bathroom Floor." This isn't just a narrative—it's an honest and necessary conversation about the hidden struggles that often lie beneath the surface of success. Saketha's goal is to tear down the pretense of perfection, revealing the extraordinary power found in vulnerability and authenticity.

This work is a vital extension of her core belief: that education and open dialogue can transform lives. As a force for positive change and a true champion for her community, Saketha Q. Adams dedicates herself wholeheartedly to making that vision a reality, inspiring others to find strength in their personal journeys.

You can connect with me on:

🌐 https://www.onthebathroomfloor.com

www.ingramcontent.com/pod-product-compliance
Lightning Source LLC
Chambersburg PA
CBHW050414110726
47899CB00008B/2714